Crisis
Of
Lust

Eliza Rose

Cover design by: Nicki Grace

Printed in the United States of America

ISBN: 9798403308649

DEDICATION

To all my friends and family who have supported me on this journey. To my fellow readers who are in for the exciting ride and the long haul. Thank you.

R.I.P. My Step Grandmother, Orneata, who always encouraged my writing from day one. This one is for you.

Chapter One

JACKSON

I can't stop thinking about the day I had Clare's legs in the air on my bed and she was screaming my name. As I drive to meet her at the *Starbucks* on 42nd street, I rehash the sweet times we shared as I mentally set up to change her last name. I am driving the speed limit, watching the other cars pass me to get to the highway. Once I am on the FDR drive, I increase the speed and lower my window. I allow the fresh air in as I indulge in the mental memory of my baby. She took her time letting me in her mind and once we were both ready for sex, I just knew it would be magical. After getting to know each other, she finally pegged for me to make love to her. I couldn't wait to kiss her delicate skin, feel the electricity between us ignite as we shared a deeper connection.

I knew from our conversations that our love was more than mental and spiritual. I aimed to please her, taste her, feel her, and protect her.

Man, her body had me memorized, she was so fine naked. It was hard to restrain myself in my entirety as I didn't want to just be seen as a freak in the sheets. She soon learned that I am more than just a pretty face and a businessperson. I made love to Clare with my eyes and with my tongue.

The way she cooed when I gave her oral, brought me to pure lust, made my dick hard. I pumped her with the essence that I was her person. Just thinking about the first time we had sex, is sending me to a place where I can't even fuck her right now. Not in public.

Although, we would be kinky if we did. Shit, there has been many times I fantasized about snatching my bookworm babe from behind the counter at B&N and sliding up in her panties. Somewhere along my daydreaming on the road, I am honked at, and the driver stuck up his middle finger because he signaled to pass me, but I hadn't noticed. I am in the middle lane, so I drive a couple more minutes to lead to the right because Exit 9 is approaching. I get to my destination in five minutes, but parking is nowhere in sight, so I drive around toward 40th street.

It's all good though, I could use the walk. On the way there, I consider texting Clare, but I don't want to ruin the surprise. Work has been keeping me busy, I know she would be outside counting the minutes until I arrive. I missed her just as much I hoped she missed me. I love her to death, and while I have loved in the past, she feels like the one.

As I stand out front of *Starbucks*, the reflection of my nerves looks back. Today is the day I make that life changing move. I gather my thoughts, having prepped for the words to impress Clare. I even looked up some context from her favorite books to add to my proposal. I straighten my tie and tighten my suit jacket. It's a little chilly but expected as it is September. I look at the time on my watch. It's 8:00p.m. The 42nd streetlights shine around me as I spin for affect. I pause at its beauty, the movie theater sign, *McDonald's* huge display, and the *Hello Kitty* store. This is our memorabilia, and this is the perfect night for her to say yes.

We had plenty date nights at this *Starbucks* location, 6 years ago we made it our permanent territory. Every year we frequent here, the minute we walk in the employees know our orders. This strip is legendary, even over on 7th avenue, visiting *Hershey store* and *M&M's* store as if we are tourists and not residents, constantly giggling and pointing at things we always see. Clare gets me every time because I tend to end up buying her all the things she asks for, from candy, mugs, chocolate, to sweatshirts. She owns all the *M&M's* sweatshirt colors, in which they should give her a gig to advertise. She just had to "get one in every color." I have a feeling she would wear one tonight because they are her "go to."

I regain my confidence, turning back to the store, reminding myself that I put in enough effort to get this far. An eager customer brushes past me and he says, "Stop staring and push on! You look great by the way." His voice was raspy and young. I turn to him as he walks through the doors. He's right. I peek inside to find my love. Clare's in the corner, engrossed in her book, "The Kat Trap" by Cairo. She was always into those erotica books. I take a deep breath, hoping tonight will go as planned.

She is wearing the yellow *M&M*'s sweatshirt with gray leggings and her tan *UGG* boots. I wanted to match her style, but work took over and I chose to come straight here. Her hair is in a long ponytail with her bangs slightly above her glasses. She flips the page as she sips her iced medium vanilla soy with whip cream latte. With Clare working in *Barnes and Noble* as the Head Cashier, she taught me a thing or two about drink labels as she also helps in the café. I take a few steps back, as I ponder entering the coffee shop. My palms are sweaty, and my heart is beating rapidly.

I take the ring out my pocket and admire it. It's a nice 5 carat rose gold ring that her mother helped me pick out. *WOW. She's going to love this! Can't wait to make her the Mrs. Miller.* I kiss the box and put it away, ready to face Clare. I'm sure she is thinking about what's taking me so long.

The smell of coffee beans is in the air and it's welcoming. I hear a barista shout, "Clare! Iced medium Caramel Frappuccino and Coffee cake."

I see she ordered my usual. Always on point with the details.

"Hey Babe," I said as I placed a kiss upon her vanilla latte lips. She smiles quickly after.

"Hey hun," Clare looks at me with a smirk. I can tell her mind is going.

"Everything alright?" I ask and take a sip of

my frap.

"Yes..." she hesitates and stares at me.

"Tell me how was your day?" I start off the conversation.

"It was good. Work was hectic as usual. But I sold the most memberships for the month. How about you?" She said as her eyes wander around the room.

Why is she so distracted? She is usually more focused than I am.

"Oh it was cool. Had to help the boss with his computer and installed new ones around the office. You know, the usual. I got dragged around the office and did some trips around the city. I think I might be getting promoted," I said as I notice a young couple sit beside us, laughing and gazing at each other. The guy wipes the girls crumbs off her mouth with a napkin.

"Mmhmm, good to hear love," she says

but not with enough excitement for my liking. I reach in to kiss Clare. A sweet, subtle kiss.

She reaches for my hands. "You see this couple? That was really sweet. Must be nice to have someone do something nice for you just cause."

Clare takes a deep breath. Her thoughts take over. "I wish you look at me that way. You don't even clean my face like our neighbor here did to his woman. The only time you admire me is inside the house. Why can't I feel cute and appreciated more…?"

I am baffled. *What is she trying to say?!* "Clare...what's s going on? I see you are falling into a mind trap. Just what exactly are you getting at?" There's a pique in my voice. The lovely couple sneaks a glance at me.

"Sit down. Please Clare." I reach out for her hand.

She snatches her hand back, obliged and rolled her eyes. "What could you possibly say to me Jackson to fix things?"

"Oh, please Clare! Don't act like you haven't been all cooped up at work, always picking up hours. You only come to my house when you feel it's necessary for you."

"So, you telling me I don't come to cuddle you at your convenience?! Don't play with me Jackson. I'm basically there every damn day and when I can't be there it is because of our work schedules. How dare you sit here and fix your mouth to say when it's necessary for me! How about when it is necessary for you!" Clare pushes her seat back.

"Clare. Clare. Clare. You know how important my work is. I'm sorry my job is currently a priority."

"And I'm not?!"

"I didn't say that babe. Relax. Let's take a breath." I didn't know Clare felt this way. *Had I been out of touch this whole time?* I can tell she is holding back tears.

"Jackson. I love you. I can't believe... I come... second to a phone, second to work, second to your mother, second to everything in your life—"

I interrupt. "Clare. Just don't do this please. I love you. Not here." My eyes start to water.

"Jackson, you just don't understand!" she says. She buries her face in her hands as her shoulders shake.

I try to grab her hand, but she pulls away. "Baby, help me understand, please...I have something to say to you..."

"I'm sick of it!" she said blinking away tears and ruining her mascara. She grabbed her coffee, and I knew exactly what is coming next.

Everything happens quickly, I could see every muscle on her face used to look at me both angry and jealous. Her eyes wet like glass as the mascara runs down her cheeks. She throws the last of her drink on me. Caught up, I toss the ring on the table, bawling, and storm out before I am the one that gets escorted out.

Chapter Two

CLARE

I am waiting for Jackson at this table, reading and minding my business as usual. When I decide to go to the counter to place my order, a guy wearing dark navy-blue hoodie, bumps into me. He asks for a tall Pike, and I stand behind him, yelling "Hey watch it! Asshole."

He takes his drink and almost spills it on me, but I back away and reach in my purse ready to use my pepper spray. The man looks at me and says, "Sorry sweetness, I'm in a hurry and I used that preorder through the app thing. Gotta go!"

Before I can get out any more profanity, he is gone with the wind. I return to my seat to read and wait for my drink and Jackson. He sounded excited when he said for us to meet at our spot. A million things ran through my mind, but I came short of what happens when he shows up.

I was just getting to the good part of the scene in this book when the barista calls out the drink orders. I get up to get them in a rush to get back to reading. Soon as I'm five more pages in, Jackson came in while his drink was being called.

Our interaction should have been more than an argument. Things seemed hazy, even with me being wired on coffee. I just instantly felt this need to be as wanted as those around me. Jackson took my approach to my feelings way worse than I expected, but I overreacted as well, given that I encouraged the audience. Throwing the drink on him, felt repulsive and empowering. I see it in movies and finally did it myself. But when he tossed the ring on the table, I felt like an asshole. Sheepishly, I became embarrassed by the entire store.

After Jackson ran out, I'm left with about 15 eyes on me. The chatter became still, phones were flashing, and all I could hear is the coffee machines as they produce espresso. I didn't even bother to yell at the millennials and generation Z's seeking to embarrass me. I just fixed my jacket and my hair and exited in a haste.

Now what do I do?

Shit! I run back to the table. Let me pick up this ring before someone else steals it. I kneel under the table to pick up the ring and put it in my satchel before heading out. I will probably mail it to Jackson or keep it in my drawer until we get past this hump. There's someone standing by the table as I bump my head rising from below. *Ow!* I say, "I'm sorry you can have this table now," as I rush toward the exit, not looking at the person as I escape.

I stand out front and catch my breath. I walk to my right, unsure of what to do and where to go. I guess I could just go home. Jackson was about to propose, and I ruined it with my dumb jealous ways! I huff and keep walking.

It's almost midnight, not that many

people around. As I beat myself up in my head, I feel as if I am being followed. There is this eerie aura and I become tense in my shoulders. Almost like I want to look back, but I am scared. There's shuffling behind me while I walk, the pacing is increasing. I squeeze my eyes shut and stop moving. When I turn around, there is a set of eyes gazing at me under a hoodie before he enters the pizzeria on the corner.

I touch the pole for the WALK/DON'T WALK signs, and take a couple deep breaths in. Strangers look at me as if I am insane. Maybe I am seeing things? I been dramatic all night so what if that was just a normal guy? Oh, or a celebrity in disguise!

Let me hail a cab. I need to get home.

""Taxi! Taxi!" I hold my thumb out and stick my leg out, hoping one stops. *I want to talk to Jackson but maybe I'll give him his space.*

After a few minutes which felt like forever,

one finally stops in front of me. *Thank God.*

I give him the address, "1863 Wilson Avenue." The cab driver says, "Right away ma'am." He winks at me.

I smile then reach to unlock my phone. The screen lit up with a picture of us. His smile, my smile, we were so in love when we took this picture. I could feel tears in my heart the longer I stare at it.

I can't help but think about how things went with Jackson. *Did I overreact? He does treat me that way. Why do I feel so guilty?*

"Ugh!" I throw my phone down.

"You okay, miss?" the Taxi driver asks, peeking through the mirror. "Yeah. I guess. I'm just a fucked-up individual who makes poor decisions in love."

He says, "Would you like my advice?"

Since he seems to be interested in my

business, I say "Why not?" Then I do the hardest neck roll cause' I'm annoyed.

He laughs and says, "Tough shell huh? Listen. I'm just a taxi driver, but as beautiful as you are I think you need to breathe. Sleep on it."

That word. *Breathe*. I instantly inhaled. It feels like I was holding my breath. He is right. I just have to breathe. Let Jackson breathe. Let my relationship...*Breathe*.

I immediately think back to the time my counselor in college told me to *breathe.* I had just lost my father and kept getting anxiety attacks. It was hard to manage my studies at a time when I wasn't prepared for his death. My mom kept in touch with me every day just to make sure I kept my cool. The counselor, Sarah helped me with breathing exercises to speak as it calmed my nerves. I haven't had that flashback in a while. It was a dark time for me, and it took years to recover from the grief of my father. A breath of fresh air felt new and healing as I just inhaled, closed my eyes and once again…*breathe.*

"Hey pretty lady, you, okay?" His head is turned to me at a red light.

"Yes, Thanks…just trying to breathe," I smile awkwardly then pick up my phone and proceed to text Jackson.

Hey babe. I know a text message isn't going to provide solidarity for my actions, especially in our most memorable place, however; I am sorry. I Love You. I hope that you can forgive me. I understand if you need time. - C

Exhale. I feel better. I hurt Jackson badly. I hope he finds it in his heart to forgive me. I check the time and as I see it's 10:30 p.m. as we pull up to my house.

"Hey Taxi driver, what's yo' name?" I ask, because he is actually a safe driver and gave me advice, I never knew I needed.

"Tyler. Why? You want my number?" He

laughs.

I think about it. *We can be friends. Right? Now I'm overthinking it!* Clare! "Ha-ha. But if you provide it, I'm open to being friends."

I give Tyler my phone so he can give me his number.

He says, "You know, if you ever need anything. A ride, or...just a friend...Don't hesitate to give me a call."

I smirk and say, "have a goodnight."

As I grab my things to exit the cab, he asks, "Wanna talk about it while we have the time?"

"Not really but I guess a male perspective can help," I say then I roll my eyes.

I tell Tyler briefly what happened in the coffee shop, in hopes he will give some serious advice. I don't know what I was looking for, but damn it sure felt good telling someone.

Tyler says, "Women always get emotional and assume someone has it better than them. Just because their grass looks greener, doesn't mean it's worth crossing over. Maybe the couple had a problem just like yours, if not worst. You could have possibly ruined things forever sweetie." He looks at me through the rearview mirror.

There is something about the way he said "sweetie," but I shake the thought and say, "Well Thank you captain obvious. But in a way, I guess you're right. I did take it too far. I need to make things right with him. Anyways...this is uh...my stop so you have a goodnight, Tyler."

I run up the steps and insert my key to go inside and head on up to my bedroom.

I can't wait to get all my clothes off. I walk to my dresser, look in the mirror and cry. *Why am I such a mess?* Jackson probably hates me. I should delete Tyler out my phone. My phone vibrates in my purse. I wipe my tears and check my messages. There's one from mom.

Are you okay hun? Call me.

Then there's Jackson.

Clare. I honestly don't know what to say to you. Yes, you hurt me. You always disrespect me and barter me like I don't put you on a pedestal outside of work. I need maybe a week. I'm sorry I have a big work project and I have to go work on it now. I Love You, Always.

Shit! Maybe I deserve this. I slide to the floor. The tears have formed again. My life...my life has just shattered.

Chapter Three

JACKSON

I hop in my Range Rover. I take a minute. Everything I wanted to happen went wrong. Clare sprung all these issues on me in front of strangers. Nah man! I'm not wit' it. I can't believe she did that. I just wanted to elevate our life. I get how she feel but she could have just said let's go home and talk about it. Home being either 1 of our houses but seeing that she spends the most time at my crib, that's cool too. I know I'm a fool for tossin' the ring like it ain't cost me an arm and a leg, but I was H-O-T! She had me fuming during a date I thought would be sweet and romantic.

My phone vibrates in my pocket. *Buzz Buzz*

I reach for it to see *Incoming Call Mark*.

"Bro. What's good?"

"Ain't shit. Just had a date with Clare. You?"

"Nun. Just tryna see if you tryna kick it with Sal and Q."

Not really, but I guess I could use the distraction. "Aight man. I'll come for a few."

"Bet. Come to my crib."

"OK. Gotchu," I said before hittin' the end button.

I guess I can go over for an hour or two then go work on my work assignment.

I put the car in drive and start to head to his addy.

Buzz Buzz Buzz Buzz

Four vibrations mean it's a text. It's probably Clare, tryna apologize. I'll check at a red light. I put the radio on and instantly Drake's "In My Feelings" is on. This my shit! I bop my head to the track and sing along…

"Kiki, do you love me? Are you riding? Say you'll

*never ever leave from beside me 'Cause I want ya,
and I need ya And I'm down for you always"*

At the red light I tell my car to read the
message. It says:

*"Hey babe. I know a text message isn't going to
provide solidarity for my actions, especially in our
most memorable place, however; I am sorry. I Love
You. I hope that you can forgive me. I understand if
you need time. - C"*

Of course, she feels guilty now. I'm at a loss
for words. I take a minute to think about my
response. I have to pull over for this one.

I pull over in front of a pizzeria, to snag a slice
before going to Mark's. I inhale then type,

*Clare. I honestly don't know what to say to you.
Yes, you hurt me. You always disrespect me and
barter me like I don't take put you on a pedestal
outside of work. I need maybe a week. I'm sorry I
have a big work project and I have to go work on it
now. I Love You, Always."*

I know she isn't gonna like that, but it is what it is. If she is going to be my wife, she has to understand how much she hurt me. We can get past this once we learn to communicate without being irrational. I just need some time; she will still be my wife. I don't want nobody else but Clare. I put the car in park and head into Antonio's Pizzeria on 34th and 7th Ave.

I take my slice and root beer to go and continue my trip. Good thing Mark is down the block from my crib. I let the music play as I take the journey to Brooklyn. The radio started talking too much so I put on *Spotify*. I search for my Drake playlist before I enter the Brooklyn Bridge.

I wonder why she hasn't responded yet. She must be sleep. Tears start to pour down my face again as I think about the engagement ring. *Dammit Clare.*

I gotta clean my face before I meet up with my boy.

Buzz Buzz Buzz Buzz

There's a text from Mark.

Where u at playboy? Oops. My bad. I meant IT boy. Since you settling down and shit.

I laugh. He got jokes. I respond,

LOL. Almost there, homie. I got another 10 minutes.

I'm speeding on the highway so I can go smoke and drink. Lord knows I need to escape.

Buzz Buzz Buzz Buzz

It's Q.

Bring some Lays man.

Before I can respond I get a call.

Clare.

Chapter Four

CLARE

It's 7:00 A.M. and the sun is blazing. My eyes adjust to the room. I reach over to check my phone. Not only did he ignore my call, he also didn't call me back.

Fuck it.

I ease on out of bed and slide my feet into my slippers. I really don't want to go to work. I head to my closet and pick out what to wear. I start pacing back and forth. *Should I call him? Nah C let him breathe.*

After a few minutes, I regain focus and pick my outfit. I settle for a black button up, blue jeans, and my black boots. As I head to the shower, I text my mom.
Hey, are you free for lunch?

Sure baby. Just text me where you want to meet.

I turn on the shower, then proceed to brush

my teeth. After a Listerine rinse, I grab my shower cap and head on in. The water is steaming hot and massaging my body. It's hard deciding where to meet up without thinking about my love and our relationship. *What if I run into him?* It is still heavy on my mind and in my heart. I can't sleep without knowing that he is okay, and our relationship is still…well, a relationship. I do love him. Ugh, I wish he would just text me. Text me saying anything. A fuckin' heart emoji, I don't care. Something.

It's like Tyler said, women are emotional. I'm not a true emotional girl, but my feelings did shine the other day. Enough about this, back to what to eat!

Maybe we should do something basic, such as *Taco Bell* or *Chipotle*. Actually, I'll just have her meet me at *Au Bon Pain*. I finish washing up, turn the shower off and grab my purple towel. I get dressed then head to the kitchen to make waffles and bacon. I text my mom the location. There's a picture of Jackson on my fridge as I reach in for the orange juice. *Maybe I'll stop by his job after work.*

As I sit and eat, I scroll *Facebook.* Jackson wrote, "I woke up still high. Work is gonna be a long day."

My cue to stop and get his energy smoothie.

After breakfast, I grab my satchel, make sure I have my keys and head out. I still haven't texted Tyler. The ride to work is 30 minutes, which gives me time since I start work at 9.

I walk to the cafe in the store and ask for a cinnamon scone and an Iced Grande Caramel Frappuccino. *Oh Jackson...*

****

My morning could not have gone any slower. When it is finally lunch time, I text my mom,

I'll be there in 10 minutes. Have to make a stop.

The clock says 1:02pm.

I head into "Nick's Health Shop" and ask for "mango, pineapple, banana, orange juice and chia seeds, please?"

Nick blends the ingredients and says, "Is this for your hottie boyfriend?"

I laugh. "Yes Nick. Damn. Why you always eyeing mine?!"

He laughs, "My bad girl. I can't help it. You know what sassy; this one is on me."

"Thank you Nick!" I grab the smoothie and rush to the cab that is waiting outside. I have about 45 minutes left for lunch. I know lately he has been traveling around the city for work so his ass better be there!

Once I arrive, I struggle with whether I should text first or surprise him. *Clare just take yo ass on!* I head into the building and the security guard greets me.

"Hi sir. I'm kind of in a hurry. Can you please send Jackson down?"

He says, "Sure Ma'am." Then he reaches for the phone, punches some numbers in as Jackson answers; the guard then says, "there's a young lady here to see you.

When he hangs up, I say "Thank you." As I am waiting, I hear chatter. It is too familiar for my ears…

"Bro she was so beautiful…"

"So why you didn't…."

Shit. *Is that Tyler?* I turn my head to hide and hope he don't see me. He continues to walk by speaking to his colleague, which he was too busy to glance in my direction.

As I am about to grab the newspaper on the desk, I see Jackson coming from the elevators behind security.

Will he be happy to see me?

He is speaking to a co-worker. I'm getting anxious as he approaches.

Before Jackson, sees me he yells, "Tyler! My man!"

Oooooohhh!

I squinch. Jackson looks at me and smiles.

"Clare. Babe, why are you hiding? Is that smoothie mine? You didn't have to..." Before I speak, I turn to make sure Tyler is gone. Instead, he is lingering by the door and my heart is racing.

"Jackson, wait. I wanted to surprise you, is all," I say shyly. "I know I didn't have to, but as your woman I wanted to bring you a sort of peace offering." I wasn't sure if Tyler could hear me, but as the lobby echoes, I had hoped that he had. "If that's okay. I'll still respect your space after this."

"Well. Thank you. I'm sure you haven't eaten. He looks at his Rolex. "Isn't it your lunch break?"

I smile bashfully. "Yeah, I rushed over here as soon as I can. I just had to see you. Here is your favorite. Nick gave it to me for free."

He laughs because he knows Nick can't keep his eyes to himself around him. He only refrains his hands thanks to me. Jackson is a fine man.

Next thing I know, my lips are touching his. I just had to kiss him one last time. He wraps his arms around me. I can feel the sexual tension rising.

"Ok babe. I have to go. Enjoy." After that passionate lip locking, I turn to see Tyler is gone. I run out to get back to work before my vagina speaks to my head and I get fired. My mom will also kill me for not meeting up.

I shoot her a text.

I'm on my way!

I race back to my mom safely. She is eating her salad. "Omg I am sooo sorry."

"Honey, I know you went to Jackson. It's okay. Tell me what's going on."

I brief my mom as quickly as I could, seeing as though I used some of my time. She tells me, "If you want your relationship to work, allow time to heal all issues. What you did today, was show him you're always around hun. I love you."

"You're right, mom. I love you too." I give her a hug and kiss her on the cheek.

It's 2:15pm and I realize I am running a little over my time. I guzzle down the strawberry banana smoothie my mom got me on my way back to work.

On the walk back to the store, I still cannot process Jackson...and Tyler? *Am I being played?*

****

I have butterflies since I left Jackson. I still cannot fathom Tyler at his workplace. *Had Jackson mentioned him before?*

Maybe I was and still am a shity girlfriend and hasn't been listening as much as I was complaining.

The rest of my workday is a blur as I keep replaying them in one spot. I am sure Tyler heard me. Maybe he was trying to see why I was there. As much as I tried to hide, there wasn't enough time to bail as Jackson came and acknowledged him too.

It was nice to see Jackson. I only wanted to give him his smoothie. I think space is working for us. Yes, I had ruined a proposal. *So why was he still being nice to me?*

That night I took the cab home, I almost eased into temptation. I used my better judgment. It's the reason I hadn't used Tyler's number to call him.

I always fuck up my relationships. But not until that one guy who broke my heart. He left me for my best friend. They even got married. So, excuse me, if I'm a little broken.

Chapter Five

JACKSON

Yo, last night with my boys was a trip. I been such a workaholic and focused on my girl that I ain't think to hit them up to chill. I'm glad Mark wanted to link. It was a good time. My boys always know when Clare messes with my head space. Rather than trying to get me to cheat, they get involved enough to tell me how to fix it or let her breathe.

Soon as I got there, they let me have it. Q was passing me the blunt, and Mark was handing me a shot of Belvedere. Sal just laughed at how they were trying to get me under the influence so quickly.

I gladly took them all and greeted them all with a dap and a hug. Then we all sat around the table, passing the blunt and playing cards. The first game we played was Spades. When it was my turn, Mark said, "So what's been going on with you two?"

I sigh. "A lot. Clare has insecurities. She thinks because I am working a lot that I don't give a fuck about us. I do, it's just to make it to where I need to be I have to grind. Feel me?"

"Yeah, I feel you on that bro. You know women be trippin' but, you have to make time for your lady. If she feels underappreciated, you have to add to that times 20 so she can function as a happy woman again."

Mark says, "Listen to Q man. You know Quentin has always been the ladies' man since high school. He got some wisdom somewhere up there in his head."

Sal laughed. "You don't need looks to understand how to love. Just keep reassuring her that she's the one and everything will fall into place.

I nod my head. I throw down an ace card.

Then it's Mark's turn. This is the reason why I love chillin' with my homies. They just get me.

Q: Let's not make this a sap session. Not gon hold you, I am tryna smoke weed, get drunk.

We laughed and got fucked up. After kickin' it, I left because work duty calls in the morning.

****

When I had arrived at work, I was not ready for the busy day. We had IT call after call. We even test run going to homes to fix computers. When I say my legs need a break, they feel like Jell-O.

Clare coming to the job was a nice touch. I hadn't expected her to be generous after our last encounter. But she knows me.

I'm not gonna lie. I posted my status on Facebook on purpose. I wanted to test her loyalty. My baby came through.

When I walked out the elevator, chattin' it

up with Tyler and Richard, she was awkward and hiding, looking nervous as if someone is watching her. I didn't question it as I just wanted to hold her. I missed her. My mind's eye chucked it up to embarrassment, fear of rejection after she played me in *Starbucks*. But I can't get over her hiding behind the newspaper.

It's 6:00pm and I'm writing down my reports for the day before leaving. I go clock out and see my boy, Tyler. He been working with us for a minute now, I say 2 years. He does ride share on the side as a backup plan and he always like to hustle. I said one day I'll invite him out with my crew. My work buddies and I usually meet up every other Friday. Maybe Tyler will come out next week.

Tyler is usually a private person, but lately he been opening up since he met "some girl" in his cab. He said he won't reveal her name or how she looks, but he knows he just has to smash.

All the jerks laugh at that comment, I just

rolled my eyes. We fist bump and then I tell him,

"I check you later kid. I'm heading out for the day."

He says, "Tomorrow my man."

I head out the doors and shoot Clare a text,

Hey, the pictures of you and mom are sweet. Thanks for the smoothie. You been on my mind all day. Hope you had a good rest of the day.

I press the button to unlock my car door.

Once inside my phone buzzes. I take my phone out, plug it into the charger and read the text.

It's Mark. *Damn.*

P*layboy. My bad we got you turnt. We bout to do it again tomorrow. Come through?*

I reply, *Bet.*

As I start to pull out the parking spot to head home, I see Clare come up on the navigation screen.

The text says,

Hey love. Happy to help. Work was fine. My mom says hello. She loves you, Jackson. Maybe we can talk one day...after your much needed space. Kisses.

I make a mental note to respond to Clare. I just want to rush home.

****

It takes me 15 minutes to get home. I hang up my keys on my key holder. Then I take off my shoes. I decide to bathe. My body hurts and my mom always told me Epsom salt, baking soda and a good drink are the best ways to heal. I walk to my little bar in the corner and pour some Jack Daniel's Whiskey in a shot glass. I doubled up so I don't have to come back for a refill. Then I head to the bathroom and respond to Clare.

Baby. Tell her I said hello. We can do lunch or dinner, whatever you want. Let me know. I just got in. I'm going to relax.

I run my bath water, nice and hot. I wish Clare was here with me so I can pipe her in this tub. We haven't made love in so long. I set my glass and phone on the tub cabby and start to undress. Once my shirt is off, I glance in the mirror. I wipe my hands on my face and breathe. Then I unbutton my pants and release them leg after leg. My boxers are the last to come off.

I ease into the tub. I rest my eyes for a few and fantasize about Clare. If only she would come over tonight. My left hand grips my dick as I stroke it thinking about the last time Clare was here with me. I picture her mouth wrapping around my shaft and doing that thang that I like with her tongue… *Damn Clare baby! Do that shit! Not too fast, I'm gonna cum!*

Almost falling asleep in the tub, I open my eyes, inhale, and exhale. *Shit!* I wonder how long

I can keep up with this space. I grab my phone and scroll *Instagram*. Tyler's profile pops up and he has a selfie in his cab. In the back is a bag that looks like Clare's. It's a pink and purple bag and I see Luna from *Sailor Moon*. Clare told me those were limited edition, but I don't stress it. Nice to see someone else has a nerdy taste like her.

After resting for 20-minutes, I drain the water and turn the shower on. I might call Clare to come over. Hell, I can make dinner. I wash up and then dry off. I walk to the bedroom, open my drawer, and grab the blunt and lighter. I take a quick pull. Then I open my towel and take a dick pic to send to Clare. I also ask her where her bag is. I know I said I wanted space to think, but after a fight, we always make up. I need to feel her.

Chapter Six

CLARE

I sit on the window bay with a glass of wine as I think about the first time, I met Jackson. He was so silly.

When I met Jackson, I was in a good headspace. I just started out at *Barnes and Noble* as a cashier. He was wandering around the store. He was a frequent customer. He walked in on a Thursday in August. I was in a yellow sundress and white flats. I noticed him often but avoided helping him.

We had made eye contact a few times. It wasn't until my boss asked me if I could help him that I knew it was a love connection.

Jackson was peeking around the horror section and asked me for suggestions. I mentioned Stephen King is a good buy. He continued to eye the books, gently touching the binds. He looks around and says,

"You know. I'm never here for the books."

I laughed. "Oh? So, are you a stalker or something?"

He walks to the children's section. He laughs and says, "I stalk the ultimate beauty baby girl." The look in his eyes showed lust and great attraction. He licked his lips on some LL Cool J vibes and I had to control myself before I felt moisture between my legs for this fine stranger.

He grabbed a basic ABC book as a distraction from my co-workers who might think I'm not doing my job.

I say, "Nice choice. Is it for a nephew or son?" As customers pass by, I try to upkeep my smile.

He whispered, "I know you gotta return back to the front so how about I take your number down. Then he looks at the book in his hand, smack it once against his other hand and says, "I'll purchase *My First ABC* by DK and you write your name on the receipt."

I nod, bite my lip, and say, "Yes sir. Feel free to browse and we will ring you up when you finish." I walk back to my work area. I tried my best not to smile.

As expected, he approached the line after 10 minutes of me working and I quickly wrote my number down. The little girl inside me wanted to scream. He was so fine. He had come in with a red button up and black slacks with shoes. His eyes spoke to my soul and almost to my drawers. So, when he asked me for my number, I had to jump on it before he decided to ask some other chick.

My anxiety was through the roof that day. I had doubts that it was all game and he wouldn't call. Why would he call a nerd in a bookstore? But sure enough, once I clocked out at 3:30pm, there was a text.

It said,

Hey Beauty. It's the Beast. Aka Jackson. ;). Nice to meet you, Clare. Hopefully one day I'll show you this Beast, but you gotta earn it. Let's go on a date. You pick the place. Tell me what to wear.

I liked his bluntness. His swag turned me on. I was way too excited for his text. I bit my lip as I walked out saying bye to everyone in view. I responded,

Hello Jackson. Nice to meet you. Beauty and the Beast is MY favorite movie! We should watch sometime. A date? Already. Hmmm... I'm basic, so Starbucks? Start off with casual coffee and conversation. Dress normal, no work stuff.

At least, he can't kill me if we are around others. I plugged my headphones in and prepared to take the subway.

He wrote back instantly,

Starbucks it is. How's tomorrow after you get off?

Of course, I said yes. Our first date was the usual 50 questions spiel. "What's your favorite color? Pet peeve? Hobby?" On and on and we both answered each one. It was cute getting to know him mentally and the thing is, he actually paid attention to my answers, almost as if he was calculating, must be the tech in him. We laughed, drank Frappuccino's, and ate banana bread.

I enjoyed his company for someone I just met. We had instant spark and I knew from my parents; you just don't let that go. Our bond increased after date number four. We became official boyfriend and girlfriend after two weeks.

Things were looking up for us as I became Head Cashier, and he'd just became head of IT at Dean & Taylor Associates. He insisted I move in with him, but I didn't. I kept my own apartment because I was taught it's best to live together after marriage.

Jackson and I have the perfect relationship. Our friends still call us the perfect couple. For a while, I believed it. But I still hold on to insecurities and they get the best of me.

I'm a jealous girl. The nights he stayed out working, you couldn't tell me he wasn't doing anything else. My friends told me I'm trippin'. I done seen it before and heard it before. Jackson always has to reassure me he was nothing like who I been with.

I calmed down for a while. I trusted him. Therefore, I have my own crib, to protect myself from any wrongdoings and I can't imagine the long hours away, living with him. When he hangs out with co-workers or his friends on alternating weekends, it is as if I have to make time. *Am I even important?*

So, before people think I'm some crazy hood rat, at least understand it's not all my fault.

Shit I'm out of wine.

I go to the fridge to pour some more wine. As I head back to the room, I think about what recently happened in *Starbucks*. I didn't mean to snap. It's just I can't remember the last time Jackson showed me that type of love. Don't get me wrong, I enjoy sex and other forms of affection. It's the little things in public, that works also.

While we have been texting on good terms, I still think we need a break. As I head to the couch, I receive his text. *Oh my!* This boy is trying to get me. I want to put my clothes on and head his way, but I'm going to enjoy some time alone. I respond,

Sorry. Too exhausted. Maybe tomorrow.

It's a half lie and the truth. I am tired. But I also don't want to be a booty call. I check the clock on the wall. It reads 8:00pm. It wouldn't hurt to rest...

Buzz Buzz Buzz Buzz

I am awakened by my loud ass phone. Kayla, my homegirl since college texts,

Girl come over. Let's gossip and drink and watch YOU.

Ugh. Why does everyone choose today to bug me!

I write,

I'll be there by 10. Need some time to freshen up. Have my glass ready!

Okay. I know I shouldn't, especially since I convinced myself to stay in, but it's not like I'm getting dick. My girls are my therapy. Jackson not about to make me feel guilty in my own home! Knowing Kayla and Calli asses if I say no, they will only just show up to my house and drag me out of bed.

I head to my closet. I pull out a red tee shirt, black leggings and red UGGS. A bitch just going to hang. I fix my hair in a bun. Then I go to the fridge to take the bottle of wine to the head. There's not much left, so I also take a shot.

I have to pee, so I use the bathroom. I check my outfit and apply lip gloss. After I wash my hands, I call a cab. *How crazy would it be if he shows up at my door? Tyler. Tonight, is not the night. I been drinking and I could get frisky.* Luckily, within 5 mins the cab appears and there is no Tyler. I inhale and confirm it's my ride before getting inside. My mind trails back to the night I met him. I'm half disappointed and half relieved he didn't show up at my door.

Jackson's text has my mind reeling and thinking about things the devil is making me do. Tyler's broad shoulders, as he has his hands on 10 and 2, his sultry eyes keep staring at me through the rearview mirror. I picture him giving me that sly smirk and his pearly whites say, "Baby I can pull over for a quickie if you like." I begin to touch my breasts and my mind trails off to him getting naked, his hazel brown eyes looking passionately in my eyes his and soft caramel skin touching mine as he smells of V.I.P. by Usher. His manly, IT and rideshare hands pull me in for a kiss as his sexy lips inch closer.

Too deep in my own head, the driver clears his throat. I stop mid imagery orgasm and say "Sorry. As you know, 44-86 41st Street please."

I open my phone to scroll *Instagram*. I look into the rearview mirror, and my driver is blushing. I silently chuckle. As I am about to comment on a Lance Gross photo, Kayla texts,

Girl are you in a cab? Calli, Sabrina and Abby are here. We waiting on you girl!

I pop the text into full screen and reply,

Yes girl! I'm on my way. Please, have a sip without me! Lol

If I know any better, I'd say Kayla is tipsy and my other 3 sidekicks are trying to catch up. My girls and I go way back since junior high. It's why I dragged my feet out the house to see them. Plus, I need my girls' insight on my complicated life. I can always count on Kayla and Abby to give it to me straight, while Sabrina and Calli motivate me to see the bigger picture. Although, at times Calli plays devil's advocate after she listens to a full story and judges it. She might just tell me if Jackson and I are single, then I should sleep with Tyler.

Anyways, the cab pulls up to my destination and I tip $5. I say, "Thank you." Then I get out to ring Kayla's doorbell. She buzzes me in. I take the elevator up three levels and head to her apartment. Before I can turn the knob, Calli is already opening the door. She hugs me and I return the gesture. She says, "Oooo I just KNOW you got some tea!"

I roll my eyes and laugh as I greet the girls. Kayla says, "I'm soooo excited you came! I know how hard it's been since you and Jackson took a break. I made you a cocktail because I need you to feel good!"

I take the glass and sniff. It smells like a pina colada, but Kayla wouldn't be that simple. I'm sure there's dark and light liquor in here. I just wanted more wine, *dammit!* I take a seat on her couch and ask them what each has been up to. As we are catching up and enjoying girl's night, I think about Jackson. I thought about texting him, but my conscious said *don't even try it. Stop being the typical woman that ass kisses to a man! Enjoy tonight.*

Facebook is tempting me to check his page. I search Jackson for his profile and that's when I hear, "Helloooo Clare. You there? Sabrina just asked you to tell us what happened after the day at *Starbucks*." Kayla is snapping her fingers in my face.

I laugh and say, "Sorry y'all I zoned out for a sec. You know how distracting phones can be. Okay so let me put y'all on to my existence. I close the app. Y'all know a girl be trippin' and I think I fucked up big time." Here goes nothing...laying it all on the table...

All of them are watching me with interest.

They knew he was going to propose before I did and now, they want to know why I messed up the moment I always wanted....

I catch them up then mention Tyler.

By the time I got to the part about Tyler there were a few *oooo's* and *aaahhh's.* Kayla says, "Girl. I love me some Jackson. Don't go fuckin' this up! You should of took that damn proposal. He loves you and sees you for you."

"You're right. I just need some time to think about it all. He's my man. But at the same time, I want the things I feel I deserve. Is it too hard to ask for more affection? Less work?"

Calli says, "Girl you single. Just get ya nut on and proceed with life. Jackson can't be mad at you!"

I laugh. She's trippin for real.

Sabrina shoves Calli and says "Pay her drunk ass no mind Clare. She's just jealous that she can't keep a man. Mind you, her last man Joe, ended up cheating on her and now she wants no part of love. Now, I agree with Kayla. Jackson is the best thing for you. Even if new dick looks good, it won't feel good the next day."

Abby spits out her drink, laughs and says, "You ladies are crazy as hell. I also agree with Kayla. He's the one, boo! I know your instincts are to fuck someone else when you think things aren't going to get better, but trust me, if you do, you'll regret it. So… Clare, have you decided on a choice yet?" Then she lifts her cup to her lips and sips some more.

I swallow my thoughts. *Do I know what I want?* "I'm letting it play out. I still do things for Jackson like give him his smoothie and we still text." Then I think quietly, *matter of fact, he sexted me earlier. I just didn't respond. He wants space, he got it!*

Kayla cuts into my thoughts and says, "Next time, send him a pic of you in your bra and panties with those red Manolo pumps and pose on the bed, with glasses in your hand since you know... you a book nerd and say some geeky shit. His dick will throb with forgiveness, and you'll get married have babies and leave us here to rot with Calli."

The girls chuckle at her assertiveness. Nothing new with Kayla. She has been this outspoken since we were in kindergarten. I remember when her mother told her it was time to leave school and go see her dad at his job, Kayla would rebuttal and say she don't wanna!

Then in junior high she pushed this boy because he was flirting with her enemy and had nerve to say to him "You're a piece of shit. Probably no good like ya daddy and ya uncle." Everyone was speechless and when the girl was going to fight her, Principal Jones stepped in and gave them detention. I could go on about Kayla, but she been my ride or die. She even stuck up for me when she thought some high school girls were trying to slut shame me for dating the lead basketball player, since they were jealous. I hear Calli's triumphant voice overcrowd my mind as she responds to Kayla.

Calli says, "Hey. That is some fucked up shit to say! But let's dance. I love y'all! Alexa, play "Please Don't Stop the Music," by Rihanna." Calli has always been the turnaround kind of girl. Trying to avoid conflict and be the life of the party. Kayla and I met her during freshman year of college and kept her after we went to a sorority party. She has been this fun ever since and knows the right time to say obnoxious shit.

Excuse me. I have to use the bathroom. I get up and walk to her bathroom. I sit on the toilet and open his text. *Man, that thing is B-I-G!*

The text says,

u miss me yet?

I'm getting all hot and bothered. After I wipe myself to pee, I sit on the edge of the bathtub and stick my hands in my panties. I use two fingers to play with myself. Before I let out a moan, I realize I need to go home. I should not be doing this in Kayla's house! It's been 4 hours too long for my blood and I have work tomorrow.

The clock says 1 A.M. When I'm done, I walk back out to the house full of smoke. coughing, I wave the weed smoke in the air. I inhale the sweet decedent scent of cinnamon, bananas, and nutmeg. That's Kayla making her munchies craving; banana bread. My stomach grumbled and I lick my lips, realizing I am hungry after all this drinking…or maybe I'm getting second hand high. I trip over a shoe that was not there the first time.

"Oouu girl, you that damn drunk? Maybe you should call it a night," Sabrina says.

"Aww man. I was hoping we could still watch *YOU*. I guess I'll have to watch it on my own without you hoes," Abby shrugs her shoulders, leans back, folding her arms.

Sabrina and Abby were a packaged deal. They joined the three of us when Kayla, Calli and I were getting drunk at a bar to celebrate our careers. Brina and Abby were doing karaoke and we cheered them on then joined them. Afterwards, we received an applause and a lifetime friendship.

"Here. Take some banana bread with you for the road boo," Kayla says.

"Clare, I hope you don't mind, but Tyler card fell out your purse, when I knocked it over and I put his number in my phone. I just might see if he wants to fool around with a free woman, rather than an almost married chic like you!" Calli laughs, then nudges my arm.

I told you, she is something else. "Geez bitches all I did was trip. But you right, I have to go. I've got work tomorrow. It's been real. Love y'all. Come gimme a hug."

We huddle in a group hug and start crying.

It's either the alcohol, the weed, the sensitivity of our convos or all three that has us in our feelings.

"And Calli. You are free to do what you like with that number. He is just a new friend." I head to the elevator and when it arrives, I wave goodbye and I call for a cab. I need the fresh air so I can wait outside. When the cab pulls up, I'm so tired, drunk, and high that I didn't do my usual confirmation. I just hear, "well hello there beautiful..."

Shit! It's Tyler!

Chapter Seven

JACKSON

After I texted Clare, I put my boxers on and lay down. The weed has me feeling so chill. I'm too relaxed for my own good. I put on some music. My playlist is on shuffle and the first song that plays is "Real Love" by Mary J Blige. I think about my conversation with the boys.

They always chop me up and tell me how to fix things. My pride got me holding off on popping up on her. I need to figure out the first and best option to move on from what happened.

Since I sent her the pic, there has been no response. *She's really pissed at me.* I close my eyes and vibe to the music. I had fallen asleep without realizing it because it is now 2:45 A.M. and I have to take a leak.

After I use the bathroom, and wash my hands, I head to the kitchen, I'm starving. The damn munchies. Reaching for the Cinnamon Toast

Crunch that's on top of fridge, I pour it in a bowl and get the 2% milk and a spoon. I head back to the bed to check my messages, chewing cereal and holding the bowl. Nothing from Clare yet. I'm tempted to text her again, but that messes up this whole process. Guess I'll just have to accept she took my space into full force. It's killing me because every time my mind says her name, I get horny. I just want to take her down in my bedroom. Hell, in the shower.

I may need to end this distance soon and get us back to that old thing. I will tell her I'll work less or work from home and accommodate more of her needs. First, I'm taking my ass back to bed. I had one hell of a night.

Damn yo! It's 3:30 A.M. and my morning wood is stronger than a muh'fucka. Guess I'm stroking it out round two! Maybe another sex tease will get her to see me. A quick hand job and there is white semen all on my hand and on my dick. It's a scene I want her to see so I grab my phone, take a pic, and pull up Clare's name. I text her,

Still yours. This is from my mind, fantasizing over you and calling your name.

I clean up then lay down and close my eyes. I can finally rest up to have energy to do this all over again tomorrow.

****

I squint my eyes as the sun beams through my curtains. I press the button to unlock my phone and the time says 6:10 A.M. I force myself out the bed to make breakfast. *French toast with maple bacon and orange juice sounds good!* I grab my red robe and put on my Nike slippers then head to the kitchen. When I open the fridge to nr the ingredients, my phone is singing out "Dear Mama," by Tupac Shakur and I head on over to answer her call.

"Hey Ma," I say as I prep breakfast.

"Hey baby. How are things going?"

"Honestly Ma, not so good. This time it's not my fault."

I put the French toast and bacon on the stove.

"Tell me what's wrong baby, I have time as long as you don't have to rush to work."

"I'm sort of a boss now, so I have time. It's Clare…" I update her on the recent events. She tells me I should have called my sisters before things got worst. "I know maybe, I'll give them a call later."

I break out into a soft cry and say, "I miss her Ma."

"Best thing I can say is, wipe your tears babe and call her. It doesn't have to be today. But stop all this nonsense! I love Clare, you guys bring out the best in each other. Do you remember the time she was nervous about her promotion, and you talked her into being head strong into manifesting she has the job? Or when she didn't think she will pass that science test in college, and you made her flash cards to help her study. How about when you were so exhausted that one day baby, and she screened all your calls by telling everyone you are taking an R&R day—"

"Aight, aight. You got it Ma. Dang. Just keep reminding me why I love this girl," I laugh then she continues speaking.

I am eating as my mama talks. I want to schedule a meeting at work, so I have to keep things moving. Then we change the subject to how her and dad are doing which she tells me they are packed and ready to head to the Bahamas. Before I can scold her on safety regulations, my doorbell rings.

"Hey Ma. I have to go; I will give you a call later. Someone is at my door. I love you."

She says, "Okay sweetie. Call me later. I love you more."

I walk over to the door and look through the peephole. It is Tyler.

How did he get here? I never gave him my address. I furrow my brows. Then I scratch my chin as I think about how the fuck this nigga get here?! Everyone at the office knows not to do no shit like that. I'll have to find a way to get him to spill it.

I open the door and say, "Hey Tyler. My man! This is…a surprise." What can I do for you?"

Chapter Eight

TYLER

I woke up ready to pitch my ideas to Jackson so we can become co-partners. I want a piece of the action. At work yesterday when he stepped out to use the restroom, I eased into his office to snoop around for his address. On his table was a letter addressed to him from his cousin and the information I needed was calling me. I pulled out my phone and took a picture so I can show up.

I made my way over to his house. This is all a part of my plan to get closer to Clare. If Jackson and I become closer at work, the more he trusts me around his homies, then maybe he can introduce us.

HA! Little does he know, I already met her. I can still smell her *Love Spell* scent from the car ride the other night. I snatched her scarf that was left on my floor and never told her I have it.

I posted the pic of her bag on *Instagram* to

rattle Jackson's brain. But he probably been so distant from Clare lately that he cannot tell that *IS* her bag.

So, I dip into playing with his mind and make my way to him at 7:00 A.M. By now he should be eating breakfast or getting dressed for work. Enough time to sit and chat because he has no choice. I walk into his apartment building and take the elevator up to his floor. I can't help but think of Clare and how many times she must've done this same route. I pressed the button to level 3 and reach his door: 3A. I smirk, get into character, and knock on the door.

"Jackson yells, "One second!" Then unlocks the door minutes later. He looks at me and says, "Hey Tyler…my man! This is…a surprise. What can I do for you?"

He lets me inside, and I play the business role. Ambushing so early in the morning has him in a state of shock. Of course, he wasn't expecting me. Jackson's eyes read as alert; I can tell he is feeling uneasy about this as he is starting to sweat. Yet, he is so welcoming.

He offers me to sit down. He squints his eyes, then pats me on the back. I can't help but wonder why he is judging me. Had he figured out that's Clare's bag in my car? Did he notice we know each other from her arrival at the job the other day? Maybe he checked her phone and seen my number. This thrill chase is intriguing and exciting me. I am getting a hard on just thinking about all the fear.

Jackson snaps his fingers as I stare off in a trance. "Would you like some water? Soda? Orange juice?"

I clear my throat, "I'll take some orange juice, my guy." As Jackson heads to the fridge, I get up and follow him. I stand beside the closed door as he is reaching in for the bottle. He closes the door, and jumps, frightened by my sudden appearance.

"Tyler…you, okay? What's this about? Don't be creepin' up on me like that. I could have killed you."

I laugh and punch his arm. "My bad. Didn't mean to make you choke."

I sit down and sip on the orange juice. Tropicana, my fav. I watch Jackson roam around the kitchen to gather his breakfast and his lunch. I tap on my glass and wait for his reaction. He almost drops his travel case of food and I try my best not to chuckle.

I spend 20 minutes inside his home, discussing the proposal and observing the pictures of him and Clare together on his fridge. "Hmm. Nice scarf Clare has on here. It's pink and says Louis Vuitton. It reminds me of the scarf I found in my car the other day. But not to worry, plenty of chicks leave their mark behind when I do rideshare."

As I'm laughing Jackson raises his eyebrows. He

says, "Yeah that scarf is pretty common. I bought that for Clare when she graduated."

"Oh, how precious," I say, unbothered. I take a piece of bacon and say, "alright buddy. I will let you finish up. I have one more stop."

I smirk on my way out the door. He asks, "Hey bro. How did you get my address?"

I laugh, quickly form a lie in my mind. The words fly out, "Oh you know… uh, I used our database at work. I was searching for Randall's surprise party invite and his address in which yours came up first. I hope you don't mind."

He says, "You could have just asked me yesterday when you saw me."

"Well…I better get going," I say as I reach for the doorknob. Actually, do you mind if I grab one of those energy drinks? I seen it while you were in the fridge. I have a long day ahead.

Jackson is in some emails on his phone, very

distracted, walking to his phone that's ringing again. Must be Clare, there is urgency in his pace. He tells me, "Do you mind getting it yourself? I have to get that."

I nod my head as he walks away and then I rush to the fridge to quickly snap a picture of them two smiling and wearing their matching M&M's hoodies and my Clare...wearing that sexy scarf. My heart is racing.

When I head to my Toyota, I put Clare's address into the GPS. *I hope she is home! It is either an off day or a late workday since those bookstores have one strict open and close schedule.* I spray my Versace for Men, hoping it will entice her. Plan #2... grab at the vulnerable woman's heartstrings...panties...or have both, why not.

I snicker then put the car in drive. I look at Jackson's window and he is watching me. I throw up the peace sign and take off.

Chapter Nine

CLARE

What a nice surprise. *Of all days, he would be my driver tonight!* "How's it going to Tyler? I was...not expecting you."

He's leaning against the car, with his left leg posted up. He has a toothpick in his mouth and spits it out. His arms are crossed as he winks at me. He laughs as if he knows I'm full of shit. He says, "You sure? You sound hesitant. I'm good boo, you know just working." Tyler licks his lips then smirks. It's sending signals to my body that are very dangerous.

As I'm walking, my legs feel loose, and I stumble on the leveled concrete. Like clockwork, Tyler's instincts have him catch me midair. His arms are on my back and as we are dipped over, in a moment that makes me feel so hot and bothered, I want to taste his fine lips. His face is close enough and we inhale. I can smell his breath; it smells like spearmint. I don't make the move. Instead, I say, "Hey, Thanks. Had a bit too much with my girls. Maybe I should sit down. Will you hurry up and get the door! Damn!"

He lifts me up and says, "You did all this to feel my hands on you didn't ya?" Then he opens the car door and chuckles. His hands...so tough and so big. So strong. He's very impulsive.

I sit on the seat and pull the door handle to close it as Tyler is also pushing it shut. I look at him and say, "Yeah, you know you're not the only driver in town, right? So why does it always have to be you?"

He taps the door and heads over to the driver's seat. He says, "It's okay. I would miss me too. I'm very good looking and patient." He looks in the mirror and smooths his hands on his face, grazing his beard. When I gaze at him through the rearview mirror, he smiles. That damn conniving smirk!

81

I wink at him then turn away. As he is driving my mind drifts to naughty, dirty, sex. I close my eyes and imagine Tyler next to me in the backseat. He grabs my hand and kisses it. Then I jump on him, and we start making out. He slips my shirt off and unhooks my bra. We are still kissing as I loosen his pants. I put my hands in his pants and feel the girth. He's got to be a size 9! It's long and slim, stern, and ready. I'm about to take my pants off and insert him inside me and straddle him…

He interrupts me and says, "Somebody had a fun night. Must have been the ladies' night. You should go out with them more often. You weren't this friendly last time. Or is it because of my handsome face?"

Was I moaning? I need to get laid.

Tyler is still watching me in the mirror as he drives. I touch my clothes to make sure I'm still dressed. My bra is loose, which I can say I was deep in my own head and hadn't noticed I released it. It feels soooo good to be free! I check the floor to make sure no panties fell. I look back at him through the mirror and he is biting his lip.

He laughs and his sexy smile is alarming. I close my legs and try to think about the trees and car lights as I look out the window. A distraction away from this.

Tyler says, "It's okay. Alcohol brings out the best...and the worst in me also. Just know if you want me to pull over, I'd be happy to please you right now..."

I cannot do this. I just can't. It wouldn't be right. But, at the same time...why do I want to? Damn, he is fine. Ugh. All this sexual energy is biting me in the ass. I laugh at him and say, "Boy if you don't just take me home with your smart mouth."

He says, "My mouth is multi-functional. Not only is it smart, but it also sends shockwaves during oral, and it finds humor in times of need.

It's professional and plump." I bite my lip. He enjoys teasing me.

I want nothing more than to feel his lips between my legs. They look juicy and I really need some kind of release. But I have to control my urges. He's not Jackson and he never will be. I take in a deep breath, trying to calm myself. I could feel Tyler staring at me and I do everything I can to not look back at him. Instead, I pull out my compact mirror and fix my hair and apply lipstick.

"You good?" he smirks. He knows what he's doing. He's taking advantage of the fact that he knows I want him. I nod and say I just need some air. He opens the window for me, and I let the wind cool me down.

The fresh scent of NYC air and the honking of horns releases the friction between my legs. I open them and hope the air makes its way there. I feel a bit moist, and no way will I indulge in answering my body's calls to give in to his temptation.

"All good, was getting hot, that's all," I start getting fidgety. I pull my phone out my purse to text Kayla. I need someone to make some sense out of this!

Girl! I'm on my way home and you would not believe who is the driver! Fuckin' Tyler. What do I do?

I wait a few minutes and figure she wouldn't respond since it's late. As I wait, I figure I make conversation. I ask Tyler, "How was your day?" Half expecting him to mention Jackson.

The GPS says 15 more mins to get to my house so this should be fun. He says, "My day was fine. I worked, rested and I am back to work again. Jackson is really a strong businessman. Gotta give it to him. I inspire to be just like him one day."

Jackson. Of course, he would say that. Tyler for sure heard me and seen me when I visited

Jackson at his job. He purposely ignored us! This little troll! I'm just glad that Jackson has been succeeding at his work. Nothing personal, Jackson's last sexy pic made me wanna go pounce on him. But I must stay true to what he asked for. It's hard, as you know I'm having all these dirty thoughts!

I look at Tyler, unsurprised just to play along with his game. "Sounds like a tough day. I hope you stop working to relax soon."

Buzz Buzz Buzz Buzz

Kayla responds:

Hey girl. I passed out once Sabrina and Abby left. Calli ass stayed over since she can get to work faster from here. I say no! I told you just wait for Jackson. He will come around. Take that ride and go lay down. Shit, use your vibrator! Don't text me on your way to work tomorrow with some crazy ass news like you woke up with him in your bed!! Goodnight love.

Dammit. She's got a point. Fine I'll just go

home like a good girl. No dick, no fun. Just sleep and my imagination. I frown then text back:

Okay okay. You know how to convince anyone not to give up the drawers but yourself! Speaking of you, I got Qs for you, so we need to link up soon. I'm almost home. I'll talk to you later. Goodnight my sweet...bitch.

Tyler looks back at me and I just smirk. I'm suddenly in a mood. I'm also starving. I open the foil with the banana bread and ask if it's okay to eat in his car.

He says, "Sure if only I can get a taste."

Those words sit heavy with me as I reply "Here. You're gonna love every bit of it." I split the piece in half and slide my hand up front to hand it to him.

He says, "Thank you so much beautiful. But I can't really grab it from you."

"So, how do you want me to give it to you?"

Tyler laughs at my word choice and says, "put it in my mouth," then he winks and blows a kiss.

The word play is sending hot chills all through my body. My kitty kat is speaking to me, begging me to end this charade with a happy ending. I silently shush it. I break off a piece of bread, inch to the edge of the seat and placed it in his mouth. He puts my fingers in his mouth, and our eyes meet in the mirror once again. This time, it says this moment is intoxicating and endearing. *I have got to get home!*

I slowly pull my hand back and ease the fingers into my mouth as if I'm tasting him in response. Then I eat my piece of bread in silence. My lovely apt is soon approaching. I drink some water quickly then make sure I have all my belongings. Last week when I got dressed for work, I couldn't find my favorite scarf. I'm unsure if I lost it in a cab or maneuvering through the office to assist my boss. I dust off my hands and my outfit then use my hand sanitizer.

Tyler pulls up to my door and I say, "Thank you, it's been real."

"Have coffee with me?"

I pause with my right foot out the door. My mind races for a response. All I got is, "Huh?"

He laughs and says, "Sorry. That was rude. Tomorrow or when you have time, will you have coffee with me? ...as friends...I swear!

"Sure. Whatever. Just let me text you okay. Right now, I'm going home to bathe and go to bed. Goodnight Tyler."

"Goodnight gorgeous," he says as I'm on my way out the car.

When I'm inside I peel off my clothes. It sure does feel good to be home. I pick up my items and put them in my bedroom. I head to the bathroom to run my bath with Epsom salt and *Sweet Pea* shower gel from *Bath and Body Works*. I light some candles and head to the kitchen naked to grab some water. I need to sober up before work.

I need to text the girls and let them know I got home safely so I go to my room and take my phone out to text the group "Bad Bitches" that I didn't fall for Tyler's bullshit, and I made it home okay. Then I toss the phone on my bed, excited to jump in the tub. I hear a loud clank that sounds like it's in the kitchen. My mind is still kind of fuzzy, but it makes me feel like someone is in my home. I wait 2 seconds, breathe quietly, and see if anything follows.

Silence.

I say to myself, "Maybe it was just the glass in the sink."

I return to the bathroom and slide into the tub. My accessories are on the table for the tub as usual, my purple rabbit and my weed. I'm not going to smoke but I will use this purple fantasy. Since it's waterproof, I stick my hand in the water and insert it inside. I press the vibrate button and it sends chills down my spine. The rabbit is hitting all the right spots and a moan slip from my mouth. "Oooo Tyler!" My orgasm is increasing, and I envision his words, "put it in my mouth..."

I start to think about what it would be like to get oral sex from Tyler. The images are very climactic and once I'm done, I inhale and exhale. I drain the tub and hear more noise...almost like my door is clicking open. Freaking out, I grab my pink towel, wrap it around me and rush out. As I put on my slippers outside the bathroom door, I swear I see a shadow in the haste, and I jet to grab my bat. I'm just paranoid, and sleepy. However, when I get to the main entrance, nothing looks touched.

Phew! Thought Tyler had followed me inside for a sec. But then wouldn't I have heard his presence or seen him before this? I think it is definitely time for bed. My mind is playing tricks on me. Tyler is on my mind. Jackson in my heart. I have got to figure things out.

In my bedroom I throw on my yellow two-piece pj's and play some music to whine down before going to sleep. After two songs, I relax and plop on the bed. My eyes shift as I am on my way to sleep, ready for the next day. This slumber is going to feel good. Something feels weird, but I don't press the issue any further. It's been quite the night. Flashing lights appear outside my window and I scream then pull the sheets over my face. Freakin' Tourist!! Why are they still around at this time?!

Chapter Ten

JACKSON

When I closed the door after Tyler left, I scratched my head. His appearance was weird and awkward for me. It's not sitting right with me. Suddenly, he wants to follow my footsteps and be my partner. I don't have much time to dwell on it as I have to finish getting ready for work. I walk to the bedroom and toss my blue suit, white button up and blue tie on the bed.

As I throw on my clothes, I grab my watch and see it is now 7:20 A.M. I hustle to get dressed so I can arrive to work at 8. When I put on my shoes, I pause. What ma said about Clare really has me thinking. I could have pushed away the only woman meant for me by being an asshole. This space isn't doing us any good besides maybe pushing us in the arms of someone new.

I hope she's still for me. I miss her terribly.

My mom is right, I have to end this. It's so

fuckin' stupid. I can't sit in my sorrows for much longer or I'll be late to work. I grab my suitcase, my thermostat, which needs coffee, and my keys. I lock up and walk to my car. In my Range Rover, I call the office to tell the team to meet me in the discussion room. Then I tell Zack to have Tyler meet us in there after 10 minutes. I want to get their opinion on Tyler's intentions before agreeing to his partner proposal.

On the drive to work, I think about the time Clare, and I had amazing sex after our third date. I took her out to Red Lobster, and we walked on the Boardwalk. It was getting dark out, and the ambiance was speaking romance. I stopped mid walk to kiss her. It was prolonged and heated. This told me she was ready for more. I looked into her eyes and told her, "Come home with me."

She said, "I don't know Jackson. I'm still getting to know you." She was frontin' on me.

I said, "Aight cool. Let's keep walking." She

94

smiled and then we held hands.

She said, "Can we sit on the beach for a while?" Then I told her, "After you my sweet princess." The area was clearing out as people were headed home. I didn't have a blanket, so I laid my suit jacket down.

She asked, "Are you sure? That looks expensive. Sand is hard to get out of clothes."

I said, "And I'm not." Then I laughed.

It took her a second to understand my corny joke before she joined. She said, "Ha-Ha. Very funny."

Then I grabbed her chin and pulled her in for a long kiss. We tongue kissed for about 5 minutes. She reached for me to pull off my shirt.

I stopped her and said, "Are you sure? Right here?"

Clare said, "Yes baby. I'm positive. Come on. No one is here and I always wanted to try sex on the beach..."

She kisses me and continue her conquest to my boxers. She says, "Take it out. I'm ready."

I pull my pants down and take my dick out my boxers. I'm ready to go.

Clare smiled, looked around and said, "To hell with it!" She grabbed the condom from her bag, which I didn't know was there to begin with then climbed on top. She rode me like she was ready to keep me. She wanted me and that's okay because I wanted her too. It felt so damn good, I didn't want it to end. The sound of the waves crashing, the moonlight stars, her beautiful face, made everything just right.

15 minutes later I came, kissed her, and told her that was beyond amazing. She cleaned herself up and said, "That was explosive! Wanna do it again?" She waited for me to respond but cut me off to say, "Relax! I am just playing! Let's go before someone actually comes."

We cleaned up, I picked up my jacket as she threw the condom out. Then we held hands and kept on walking and talking. We got to know each other that night.

I zoned out into this memory so bad, I was stuck at a red light and cars kept honking at me, cursing me out as they passed by. I pull into *Starbucks* drive-thru and order an Iced Venti Vanilla Latte, since I need the extra fuel and hand the nice lady my thermos. After paying, I wait for my order, I tell her "Thank you," and tip her $4 after she hands me my drink. She smiles and I take off.

I'm 5 minutes away from work so when the light turns green, I smile, thinking about Clare and speed to the parking lot to start my day. Man, that's a great memory! I wonder if she remembers it. No time to ask, I must get this show on the road.

Chapter Eleven

TYLER

Leaving Jackson's apt, he has no idea that I don't give a shit about anything related to work. I needed a plan to get what I want. Seeing Jackson was the perfect way in to getting clues on his current status with Clare. I also wanted to confirm that they do not live together.

In Jackson's home I captured the pics on his fridge of Clare because she's supposed to be mine! I head straight to Clare's apt and stay outside. If I ring the bell, she will ask the same questions Jackson asked. Two lies in one day is hard to keep up. I decide to study her routine so that the next time I show up, I can come at the perfect time. I went behind the nearest tree that gives me access to her home to observe her. She looks so sexy naked.

It's 7:25 A.M. when I see her wake up for work and get dressed. She took her shower when she got home from her friend's house. I start to think about feeling her. My penis is getting hard, and I have to cut my thoughts because there is no way for me to get it down the way I want to. She's walking around, I guess air drying, since she bird washed, and I snap a few quick flicks. I continue to watch her as she finally gets dressed and I leave because work duty calls! Plus, she will recognize my car quickly since she's been inside it many times.

When I dropped her off last night, I did leave. I know she was fantasizing about me last night. I'm not shallow, confident yes. But I do know when I'm wanted. I saw her daydreaming. Had to be about me... very flattering.

She was drunk and high. Not a man to take women under the influence and have my way with them, I just kept my cool. Of course, I did some teasing during the ride to her house just to see how far it will go. I wanted to pull over and give her what she wants. I know she wants me.

Then I had an idea. I wanted access to her house so that way I can snoop around. So, I turned around and caught someone fixing the doorway. Must be the Superintendent, I quickly asked him if he can do me a favor and make me a key copy as I just moved in with my sick sister Clare. I told him she approved it that morning with his wife. He looked at me suspicious and said "Alright." He reached in his pocket and handed me the key. I said, "Thank you," and took off.

This time, I didn't want to be seen using her key, since Clare is friendly and I'm unsure if she speaks to her neighbors yet so when she thought she was going to lock the door, I distracted her and told her she had dropped her earring. While she searched the porch for it, I slipped a pin in the door to hold it open and waited until she was in the bath to sneak inside. Then I checked to make sure the actual key copy works, and he didn't doop me and change the locks. I checked my surroundings and walked in.

On my way in, I tripped over her shoe. *Fuck!* I move it aside and freeze in place, waiting to see if she will get out the tub, but she didn't. Well, that'll keep her aware. I walked to her bedroom, searching for I don't know what and peeked in the bathroom and snatched her panties off the floor, they smell so good I need keep them. I pocket them then disappear before she sees me. I figure with her being high, she will see it as hallucinating rather than me actually being here. The aroma of *Sweet Pea* has been pushing me to enter the bathroom and feel her up, but that would turn out for the worst.

She has every right to her endeavors. I am sneaking back toward the entrance when I hear, "Oooo Tyler! Damn this man is sexy."

I press record on my phone, dip down to the floor and do my best to record her in action. Then when she hit that climax, she really let it out, "Ooooohhhh Yes Tyler!!! Don't stop! "

I grab what is good enough for me to use as

bribing to get in her juices, then race for the door. Outside, I snap two more pictures and my flash was going off. I curse under my breath because I am not trying to get noticed. I toss my hoodie on and escape before any neighbors or people in passing label me as a creep and call the cops.

Just have to make my next plan to get me inside of her.

Chapter Twelve

CLARE

Ugh! The brightness of the sun is radiating through my curtains, telling me it's time to start my day. My alarm ringtone sings, "Party In the U.S.A" by Miley Cyrus. My motivation to get my ass up and ready for work. I am sluggish from the little sleep I got from hanging out last night and my night cap in the tub. I get up and put my feet to my floor, shuffling around for my slippers. I yawn and stretch then grab my robe to head to the kitchen to make breakfast. I'll be quick and make a bacon, egg, and cheese on a roll with chamomile tea.

After I make breakfast, I sit at the table and check my texts. Sabrina texts me privately saying,

Girl! You were so fun last night! I can't wait to see you again. You needed that outing. I know Calli a little crazy, but you know she means well. Call me, or any of us if you need us before Friday. Enjoy your

day!

I laugh and text her,

LOL! You are too much! I had fun. I hope there is no drama today. Love you and see you gals this weekend!

I look at the clock and the time says 8:00 A.M. I have to get ready for work. I clean up then prepare for my day. I have to be at work by 9 A.M. so I get dressed and grab my purple purse.

As usual, I call for a cab. It takes only 25 minutes to get to work. When I arrive, I inhale and walk inside. Immediately upon my entrance as I'm heading to clock in, Nicole, one of the cashiers in the cafe told me that a handsome young man came in here looking for me. My arm hairs spiked up as she keeps talking.

She describes him as caramel skinned, short Caesar cut, and a goatee with a white button up and blue slacks. She said his smile was sexy and he smelled like "Usher's V.I.P...." we said in unison. I am starting to feel ill and run to the bathroom as my body is heating up and I feel sweaty.

A cheery Nicole behind me shouts, "Hey, are you okay?! How did you know that? Well, I'll see you later..."

In the bathroom, I look at myself in the mirror and grab a paper towel, wet it and wipe my face. No way. No way. *How did he fuckin' find out where I work at!? Did Jackson mention it?* I pull myself together and finally clock in. I smile and pretend as if everything is going to be okay. I greet the other employees and open my register. Once I'm ready to go, I shout, "Next! I'm open! I can help the following customer."

****

On break, I text the "Bad Bitches" group.

Girls! Tell me why I came to work and Nicole, one of my co-workers told me Tyler stopped by looking for me. What. The. Fuck. If any of you hoes, especially

Calli; texted him when y'all was fuckin' drunk and high, fess up now! So, I can come kill one of y'all or all of you. Lol! This is madness. When I say I was shook...I was SHOOK! Had me checking every customer making sure he didn't end up at my register.

For lunch I'm eating a croissant and drinking an iced vanilla latte. I have 10 minutes left and see the weather is 80 degrees. I go outside to enjoy the heat. There's a bench available, so I take a seat. I look down at my cell to respond to Kayla who has responded to my text.

She writes,

Oh no girl. That is so crazy. What's the tea though? How you have two men and not givin up the cookies? Lol Call me when you get off work.

As I'm responding back to let her know I will call her, there is a shadow clouding my view, and the stance is familiar. I look up, "Hey...Jackson. What a surprise." I smirk and look him up and down.

He smirks and says, "Clare. I missed you so much. Then he grabs my hands and reach for me to get up and embrace him for a hug. His body feels so nice and comforting. "What brings you here, babe?"

He says, "Well I spoke to my mama, and she told me I'd be a fool to lose you. I didn't want to waste any more time, so I figured I'll talk to you." He's gazing into my eyes.

"Tell, mama she's very sweet! I'm glad she checked you, ha. But... not to cut this off, it's just I have to get back to work to relieve the next worker so they can go on break. Just call me when I get off or text me okay? I love you." I kiss him on the cheek and that's when I see it.

Tyler's Toyota Camry. He is sitting in the driver's seat with this evil glare. We make eye contact for a quick second, and he speeds away before Jackson turns around.

"Wow. That screeching is hard on the ears.

Homie need to chill out before the cops pull him over."

I start to get fidgety, and my throat is dry. I need to get some water A.S.A.P. I am breathing hard and clutch my chest, reaching for the bench to sit down. Jackson asks, "Clare, honey...you, okay? You look like you just seen a ghost. Come let me escort you back to work."

I close my eyes and inhale the fresh scent of trees, as Jackson pulls me up and puts his arm around me. Once we are back in the building, he walks to the cafe and asks for "Ice water, please" and hands it to me. He kisses my forehead and squeezes my hand.

My hands are shaking. I should not be this torn apart. Maybe my paranoia is from the sounds I heard overnight. Everything is making me scared. I say, "Thanks" and walk back to my register. I tell Chloe she can go on break.

Jackson winks at me and whispers he'll call

me. He watches me ring up two customers then leaves. When the rush slows down, I feel like I'm going to be sick. I ask Nicole to watch the area while I run to the bathroom.

Whew. Clare. Just breathe. The nausea calms down as I take 10 deep breaths. I turn on the faucet and toss some water on my face. My eyes are closed and when I open them, I jump at the onsite of Chloe.

She says, "Girl. My bad, didn't mean to scare you. Are you sure you're, okay? You been flustered since you came back from break."

I laugh, hoping she can't tell it's fake and say, "Yeah girl. I'm so good. Just dehydrated. Plus, my man Jackson came to see me after some time apart from our busy schedules...he always gets me hot and bothered." I back up to the exit and touch the handle to make my way out. Only 4 more hours to go.

Chapter Thirteen

JACKSON

When I arrive at work, things seem to be running smoothly. My assistant Kevin, advise me that the meeting is all set up. I walk into the room ready to discuss the weekly updates and Tyler's latest news. Everyone but one agreed in him joining the team. I take notes on everyone's concerns then call Tyler into the meeting.

Tyler enters with donuts from *Dunkin Donuts* and has his proposal ready to incorporate more business revenue for name of IT company.

I say, "Someone came late today, where the hell you been?"

Tyler says, "Oh I stopped by the *Louis Vuitton* store to look at their belts. I have to up my game after this meeting. Now are we ready?"

I laugh. Not sure I trust that answer but fuck it.

We all nod in agreement. He is very convincing. I have no choice but to like him. I start to drift; Clare is heavy on my mind. Back before things got hectic around here, I used to meet her before work, we share a coffee together and some laughs. I would do it every morning just so her day can start off with a smile. When the work required more of me, I had to lessen that by doing early mornings in office. But, since understanding her pain, I consider going to her job to make peace. We have to overcome this...That's my baby.

Tyler is wrapping up his narrative and I stand to close the meeting. I adjust my jacket collar, clear my throat and say, "Thank you Tyler man. That was a well thought out presentation." I look around at the colleagues and tell them they are free to go. When everyone scatters, I check my watch for the time. It's going on 10 o'clock. I'm going to do a couple jobs then head on over to Clare.

****

I didn't know what to expect when I pulled up to her job. When I got there, she was on break. Today she seemed antsy. My mind couldn't grasp if it was because of me or something at work. When I mentioned speaking to Ma, she didn't respond much, and she usually loves when I bring up talking to her. Her mind was elsewhere. When we were about to depart, she stumbled and looked like she seen a ghost as she reached to sit back down. I know I heard screeching from a car behind me and it had me question is someone after her? It made me want to protect her even more. When I took her back inside and grabbed her some water, I kissed her goodbye then headed towards the door.

What Clare doesn't know is that I lingered nearby for a few more minutes. Nothing seemed strange so I went back to my car and headed back to work. The rest of my workday is going to be difficult now because that's all I'm gonna think about.

*****

I arrive back at work and Tyler is at my desk. He has a pen and pad with names of our clients on it.

He says, "Boss man. These places need more computers. Also, a girl named Alexa called from P.S. 285 stating that their educational system could use an update to their computers or even new computers since the kids cannot function with the old bots and we are in 2019. Her words."

"Well aren't you prompt today. We will plan a day to go to the school and check everything out. Then we will work something out with the principal on updates."

My phone line starts ringing and we both glance at it. Kevin is in his office across from mine and he picks it up.

His hand gestures show that it's our boss on the line. I look at Tyler and say, "I'm gonna have to take this, we can pick this up later. Have Kevin reach out to the school and if you're done for the day, you may go home."

Tyler nods and exits just as I grab the phone.

"Jackson speaking. What's going on Dean?"

After this call, I'm heading out to go home and smoke a long blunt.

****

Dean called to tell me that I'm progressing very well as a CEO. He said that he spoke to his team, and they think I'm ready to be added to the Board of Directors. I'm speechless as I hear this news. He said while I just considered Tyler as a partner, they believe he can be the new CEO and I can train him.

"Are you sure boss?"

"Would I lie to you Jackson? Come on, you're our main guy. We kept an eye on you for a while now. We think it's time," Dean says with joy in his tone.

"Okay. In that case, I'll accept. Thank you, guys, so much. You have no idea how much this means to me." I jump up and fist pump in excitement. I just have to tell Clare this now. Dean tells me they will talk to me in person in two days. I tell him I appreciate it then we end the call. I buzz the intercom to tell Kevin that there will be some changes real soon.

It's time to get ready to go home so I close my files and turn my light off. I lock the door and let Kevin know we will talk in the morning. After the ride in the elevator, I text Tyler,

Boy! I have some exciting news! Matter fact I'm bout to call you.

When I am at my car, I press the keys to automatically unlock, get in and tell the car to call Tyler. He yells over the loud background.

"Hey man, what's good?" Tyler says.

"Yo, T. Dean called me and said he's promoting me which means you're getting my spot. Sucks because I almost looked forward to you as co-CEO," I laugh.

He's silent a second before he says, "Aye, congrats homie. That's huge. Can we talk later though? I'm kinda on a date."

I pull the phone away from my ear to look at it then put it back. "A DATE!? With who?"

Tyler says, "That gorgeous girl I told you about. Aight, imma holla at you later." He laughs.

I say, "Aight fam. Later."

I put the car in drive and text Clare,

Baby Girl!!! Don't I have some news for you! Ya, boy done come up! I'm going to see if she's home to tell her in person.

I'm so excited to share the news with Clare. Instead of getting to her home in 20 minutes, I make it within 15. When I pull in front, I put the car in park and grab my spare key. I walk in and it is quiet.

"Clare! Clare...?" I'm walking around and calling her name. I look in her bedroom, to find it empty. It's weird she's not home from work.

Could she be...*with him?*

For half a second, I assume she is with Tyler, but I shake it off because they don't know each other well enough to hang out. Just the way he brushed me off too quickly and the fact she isn't picking up, has me on edge.

An ex played me that way once. She ignored all my phone calls and texted me 2 hours later to tell me she stayed late at work. Then I found out she was cheating on me with my high school friend Levi. I overheard him bragging about her twat in the cafeteria the next day. I confronted her, embarrassed her, and told Levi he can have her because it's not in my character to date hoes. Then I stormed out the lunchroom with Q and Mark following behind me. The past is long gone, and I trust Clare. I head outside and lock up. I unlock my car with my automatic keys and get inside. I press the keys on my phone to call Q.

"Hey Q, what's good? You home?"

"Jackson! Homie! Uh, yeah, I actually just got in from seeing shawty. Pull up."

"Aight. Have the Henney ready cuz I got some news for you. After we can phone in the rest of the squad," I say as I put the car in drive.

"Aight bet. Did Clare get her shit together and say she accept your proposal?" He laughs.

"Nah man. Her and I aren't there yet. This is about work. Listen, hang tight. I'll put you on when I get there." Afterwards, I hang up to vibe to music.

I call Clare one more time before hitting the *Spotify* button. She still doesn't answer. Something isn't right, I can't shake this feeling. The first song on the playlist is "We Fly High," by Jim Jones. Perfect song to celebrate me.

Chapter Fourteen

TYLER

I hadn't known what to expect when I had saw Clare this morning from outside. The curtains are always open, almost as if she is inviting me. She gave me permanent thoughts for the rest of the day as I have to act as a professional in front of her noob of a man. He is such an IT nerd; I can see why she is struggling. He is in love with his work, takes things way too seriously.

When I flew the scene to rush to work, I needed a plan to visit her job. First, I attended my own. I had to play this partner role until Jackson trusted me enough so I can start my devious plan to steal his woman right from under him. Once I arrived at work, I greeted my fellow colleagues and headed to my office. I sit and swivel in my black office chair, plotting on a way to get to Clare's job. How can I get this information without sounding like a creep?

Jackson's office! Must be a picture somewhere.

While everyone went to the main room to start the meeting, I snuck into his office. Jackson hasn't arrived yet so; I quickly scanned his room. There is a picture on his bookshelf. They are locked arms, kissing in front of Barnes and Noble. She has a name tag on that says, "Head Cashier." Based on the headdress outside of the store, and the Chase bank logo in the reflection, I believe I know exactly which one she is at. I jump for joy then quickly leave to make a store run.

****

It would be today of all days that Jackson has the same intention as I do. He is already here, coddling her. I arrived late because I went to the wrong location. An employee at the other store directed me to this spot and I hit the gas to reach it asap. First, I walked in, and explored. I had hoped I could speak to her. She wasn't around for some reason. I asked an employee where she was, and they said she was running late.

I cursed under my breath and left. I went to *Dunkin Donuts.* I see Jackson when I decide to revisit during a normal break hour. Just my luck she was outside sitting on a bench and his frame was right there. I hit my hands on the steering wheel. *Dammit!* When they embraced, she glares at me. I give a sly smile then put the car in drive, pulling away as fast as I could before Jackson noticed me. I just scared her shitless. There goes the rest of her workday.

The rest of my workday was a façade. I brought the donuts into the meeting in the nick of time and pleased my co-workers. Then I went to Jackson's office, acting interested and invested in improvements to fit in. I can't lie, I'm enjoying this IT job more than I thought. Even ridesharing has gotten fun. When I discuss work with Jackson, he is impressed with my knowledge since I usually goof around. Sadly, Jackson's boss had called and interrupted our office meeting.

I leave to return to my office to pack up. As

I'm packing my work bag, my cellphone is vibrating. I reach for it and see a number I don't recognize. I let it go to voicemail. Then I hit the play button and it's a female...not Clare. Her name is mentioned.

The message says, "Hey...Tyler. This is Calli...I got your number from Clare's bag. I hope this isn't awkward. Maybe you would like to actually fool around with someone single. Call me? Okay bye."

I frown. Then I head to my car. I'm going to pick up Clare from work.

Chapter Fifteen

CLARE

I leave work once my relief comes in. I put my headphones in, expecting to take the train. I only walk 2 blocks before I see Tyler's car. I could turn around and take the long way to the subway, but I don't. I'm interested in why he is waiting for me. I swallow, hard as if my thoughts are in my throat ready to be digested. Fuck! I pull out my Fiji water bottle and sip some water then breathe in and out before approaching him. Time seems to be against me as he has this stupid smirk while holding the passenger side of his Toyota Camry open. I approach him and turn my head to make sure no co-workers can see me. I reach him and before he speaks, I belt out, "What the fuck are you doing here?"

He laughs. *Why am I always so damn comical to this guy?!* Then he grabs my hand and says, "I just figured you needed a break from the MTA."

I blush. *Quit it, Clare!* "How nice. But before I'm convinced, you're not trying to kidnap me, explain my lunch break." I fold my arms and squint my eyes for effect. I snatch my hand away just in case I see Nick or someone nearby. Nick smoothie making ass will tell Jackson in a heartbeat.

Tyler puts his hand in his pocket and says, "Alright..." He puffs out air and says, "I had found your information snooping through Jackson's office at work. I thought I could surprise you as a friend and treat you to lunch, but looks like he beat me to it..." He smiles real big.

"Cute and creepy all at once. You could have just asked. Those rideshare apps keep track of our numbers!"

"I know...but chivalry isn't dead over here precious. Shall we?"

I don't want to believe him but I get in the

car. It's probably the worst idea, but I am having anxiety about being seen as if paparazzi is following me. It's weird being up front as I'm usually in the back. I feel like we are going to stop at a red light next to Jackson! Or one of my nosy co-workers. My nerves are shot, but I refuse to let him see that. I fasten my seatbelt and pull my phone out from my purse and with sweaty palms I text Kayla,

Girl, Tyler is up to no good...or maybe he is working his charm. He picked me up so if I end up missing tomorrow, you'll know why. When I figure out where he is taking me, I'll text the group.

When I look up from my phone, it almost slips from my hand, and I catch it in a juggle of both hands. Tyler is leaning over, staring at me. He says, "Are you going home darling? Or shall we go out for a drink?"

I probably shouldn't, but I respond, "Just one drink Tyler! Then take me home. I'm not playing with you. Like deadass."

He smiles and his dimple shows as he puts the car in drive. He says, "As you wish… sexy. Tell me. How was work?"

I laugh. "Work was fine. Typical workday. Jackson coming was a nice touch. My co-workers were looking at me funny thanks to you coming before my man...or ex man...whatever we are at the moment…showed up after you."

Tyler is at a red light, so he turns to me and says, "Aw I'm not sorry sweetums. I just wanted to talk to you. Didn't know you couldn't have male friends visit you."

I playfully punch his arm. "First of all, we are more like acquaintances. You're Jackson's co-worker and a rideshare employee that I happen to always get as a driver. I shouldn't have 5 starred yo ass."

We laugh in unison. He says, "If that's all I am then why are you in my passenger seat, not in the back as usual and why are you going out for drinks?" He bites his lip.

Damn him! Talking to my soul, sensually. I turn away before we skip drinks and head somewhere we shouldn't. I tell him, "You think cause you work in IT, you have a way with words nerd? Take me to *On the Rocks* that's on 10th Ave."

He looks at me and says, "No baby. I'm just good with my mind, mouth and tongue."

I turn away to look out the window. The people rushing on the sidewalk distract me from what Tyler is trying to do on my left. I wonder why New Yorkers always speed walk no matter the time. Why don't we ever slow down except to sleep, drink or smoke. I chuckle at my thoughts.

Tyler laughs and I'm sure he thinks I'm thinking about what just happened. He puts music on from his phone and the first song to play is "Chris Brown's, Loyal."

"Turn this shit up!" I say as I grab the knob for the volume the same time as he. The spark in our hands is electrifying.

"Sorry," We both say. The rest of the ride to the bar is spent singing in unison.

******

Once he found parking, I unfasten my seatbelt. I grab my things and open the door to get out. I wait for him to leave the car as well. We walk the 3 blocks over to the bar. I make sure to keep my distance while walking and ask him, "So, how was your day? Let's invest in you for a change."

He looks at me and says, "It was great. I had a presentation at work and Jackson seemed impressed. We are going to be partners!"

I tense up, but don't say anything except "Cool. **Congrats.**"

We finally reach the bar, and he opens the door for me. "Thank you."

"It's no big deal. I gotchu girl."

I scan the bar for the perfect spot to sit. Since it's only 5pm, there's a few after work strangers enjoying their company and their drinks.

We decide to sit at the bar. The bartender approaches us and asks if we are ready to order. I look at Tyler and he gestures for me to go ahead. I say, "I'll take a Manhattan please."

He nods and says, "And for the gentleman?"

Tyler says, "Just some of your finest and strongest whiskey please."

I say, "Don't get too crazy. I need my cab ride home." We bust out laughing.

The bartender turned and made our drinks. I was about to ask Tyler a question when his phone rang. I peeked over and seen Jackson. He tries to cover the phone and pushes it to his chest.

He says, "I'm sorry. I have to get this. I'll be quick."

I nod. "Sure thing." I wave the bartender over

and when he gets here, I say, "I'll need a whiskey shot as well. Thank you so much."

This afternoon is going to be interesting. The bartender comes back with our drinks and I down the whiskey shot. I wink at the bartender just as Tyler comes back to his chair.

"Welcome back," I smile.

"Did you miss me?" He winks.

Ah, there he is...that sexy, charming Tyler! I shake my head and laugh at him.

He grabs his drink and says, "Cheers."

"Cheers boo." We both sip at the same time.

"Oh, I made it to boo stage huh? Man, you work fast. I was just an acquaintance in the car. Even though I knew that was a lie."

"Oh. My. God. Shut the fuck up Tyler!" I'm feeling this drink already.

Chapter Sixteen

TYLER

Jackson is a good boss man and hard to persuade. During my presentation, I can tell he was doing some thinking. I knew he would come around because I'm a lovable guy. I think I aced it when I brought him new work, potentially a refreshing business opportunity that no one thought of. I am bored and need excitement so when I pack up my office for the day and decide to see Clare, I am hopeful she will accept my invitation.

When Jackson told me that I did a great job, but he is being promoted, it had my blood boiling. Why does this company gloat on him so much? I thought I had a good thing going. Working so close to Jackson had been the key to getting what I want out of Clare. Maybe when I show up to pick her up for work, she will open up to me. There is nothing a woman loves more than a man that listens...Am I right? Word on the street is that they are having relationship problems. This is the addition I have been waiting for to slide on into her bedroom.

I'm drawn to her; her beauty is infectious. It didn't take long to get to her job. I'm a fast driver. I park and wait for the right moment to charm her as she gets out at 4pm. At first, she isn't happy to see me. I bet she expected Jackson after all their little drama. She gives me a smile and it isn't as convincing. My conniving smile in return baffles her as she inches closer to me. I get in the car and start the ignition.

I smirk at the thought of her seeing my concern for her. She lays her head on my shoulder and tell me how horrible things have been lately, and how she wish it will all go away. A door slams and my trance is gone. It's Clare getting in my car on the passenger side.

I glance at her, wanting to touch her hand...her thigh...her cheek...but I don't. In the back of my mind, I thought about the message from Calli. She can be another pawn in my chess game, although she is not needed. I could use her to get to Clare. I have these devious thoughts as I drive to the bar she requested, On the Rocks. Clare's inquisition on my activities interrupts my thoughts. We have some small talk along the way, and I use my charm to sway her mind. This will lead her to being more vulnerable to me when we are at the bar, enjoying one another's company.

Shortly after we pick our seats at the bar my phone rings and it is no one other than her man, Jackson. I try to hide the name, but she sees it. She turns away and doesn't say a word, but I know her mind is going off. What does he want? It's after hours. I excuse myself and go talk in the bathroom. After a quick work talk, I head back to my beau. I start the conversation trying to get to know more about her.

I've made a joke to her, and she nudges my arm with her little fist. I take her soft play fighting as flirting. The girl only had one Manhattan and is acting so different from the woman who be in my backseat tossing slander at my flirtatious behavior. It's hot. It's cute. I want to kiss her juicy lips, but now is not the time. I must get inside her head. See where she thinks she and Jackson are in life, not that I truly care.

"So, Clare, tell me about yourself besides work, being in my backseat and falling for me," I say and sip more of my whiskey.

She chuckles. "You know what? I didn't come prepared for an interview." She rolls her eyes, jokingly. "Well, I'm an avid reader, that's why I love my work. I'm a hopeless romantic, plan to be married with kids one day. I have a tough group of friends that keep me in line. Jackson and I... we... he... maybe I..." she's stammering, half due to the drink, other half because she's stalling what she really wants to say.

I wave the bartender over. He is wiping the counter as I ask for " two shots of your strongest whiskey, please." Clare shakes her head no, but I ignore her. She needs the liquid courage to tell me what is obviously, a huge deal.

"Trust me," I grab her hand in mine and make eye contact.

She inhales and says, "I think I have to use the bathroom. Watch my bag for me?" She stumbles getting off the bar stool and I help her, still holding her hand. Clare looks at me, smiles and says, "Thank you," before releasing her hand to walk away. Her phone buzzed so I assume she is going to do what I just did.

As I wait for her to return, I look around. Quickly, I slip an ecstasy in her drink. Everyone is in their own drunken world, deep in laughter and chatter. No one notices as I look through her purse, unsure of what I'm looking for. Her work ID is just as sexy as her state ID. I notice the card I gave her is missing. Calli. The name comes back to me, and I make a mental note to call her later or tomorrow. There's a paper sticking out, like a journal entry but I can't pry any further because I hear those heels clacking. Clare. I quickly turn to my drink and stare at the wall of second shelf varieties.

"Did you miss me?" She throws my words back at me. Damn she's hot. She sits back on the stool.

"Actually, I did. I thought you might escape through the bathroom window or something," I joke.

Clare spits her drink out, bursting with laughter. "Sorry, I had to pee so bad. Then I had a missed call from Jackson. I was going to call him back, but he can wait. I did text my friends, just in case...you know...you kidnap me." Her eyes are giving seduction.

I wink and place my hand on the small of her back. I inch closer to her ear and whisper, "Baby Girl, I won't do anything you will not allow. Like how close you are letting me get to you during this wonderful, eventful afternoon." I lick her ear.

She is breathing hard. "Tylerrr..." She moans. "Can I... finish telling you what I was gonna say before I went to the bathroom? Although, none of it matters right now." She takes out the paper in her purse and fans herself.

"Sure. Let's take these shots. You, my dear, are going to need it more than I do."

We tap the shot on the table, tap the glasses together and stare at each other as we down them.

"Okay so what I was trying to say is after that night you picked me up...I gave him some space. He started opening up and sending texts. It's just me...wait why am I getting so hot?!" She is rambling, stammering, and starting to feel the shot, only a matter of time before the drug kicks in.

I watch her as she continues speaking.

This time she speaks fast as she says, "I didn't

like that he wanted space, but I kept that up no matter how many pics he sent to me. Very hard, tempting, I almost wanted him to come over to make up...sorry if that's TMI..." She stops, to breathe and order a whiskey sour.

I nod my head. Inside my head, I roll my eyes. I could care less about this, but I'm doing my best to get to know her. To avoid my plan getting blown, I express fake worry. So, I touch her arm with a look of concern. "I get it boo. You love that man." I swallow. It's hard for me to say that.

She says, "I had only wanted to make him feel the pain of what he asked for.... he showed up to my job, being all sweet and now I'm...I'm confused." Clare almost falls off her chair.

I catch her by the hips and say, "would you like some water?" She nods. I order the water and say, "So what I'm hearing is that you pretend like you don't give a shit, but you actually do. You are a hard worker, committed to your job and your lover, and a great friend. Interesting qualities my beautiful lady." I smile. "Wait are you okay? Your face is flustered, you're stumbling, mumbling, maybe we should chill out on the drinksss…?"

There's a warmth to her. As I sit, getting to know her I am even more pulled into her. "Clare bear, what do you like to do for fun?" I say with an evil grin.

She giggles, "Eeww. What an ugly nickname. I like to read, draw, and watch tv. How about…how about you? Your nose looks funny!" She chuckles and takes off her jacket. Her boobs are looking delicious.

Hm. *What do I like to do? You soon, Clare bear.* "I like to work. I love long walks and good conversations. I too, watch some tv. I like to drink, clearly so do you; miss one drink only turned three." We laugh together.

She says, "Oh yeah. You are so right about that. How the hell did I get this far? Damn you, Tyler! Truth be told, it's been kinda fun. Thank you. Thank you. Seriously, Thank you!"

The unthinkable happens next.

I say, "You're welcome" and before I can say anything else she embraces me with a hug. Ah, sweet scent of *Sweet Pea* from Bath & Body Works. The same scent that's locked on the panties I stole when she was in the bathtub.

The hug is tight, secure, and sexy. I think she is starting to feel safe with me. Great. When Clare pulls back, I grab her butt. Her body feels limp, and she gives me a hazy smile as she gazes into my eyes. A minute too long and she kisses me. Inside, I'm in shock. I'm excited. My cock is ready to take off. We had one too many drinks. *Is this a tease?*

There is random cheering around the bar. They must think we're a couple. My tongue slips in between her lips and my left hand finds her hair and holds her head.

She pulls away after a while and says, "We

should probably goooo."

I glance in her eyes, as usual, I tell her "Sure. Let me get the tab."

****

I take my car keys out, ready to drive her home. Clare smacks them out my hand and says, "Oh hell no. You are not killing me tonight. Call a cab."

She's hilarious. I have drove around many times after two drinks. For her safety, I'll call her a cab home. I told her, "Alright fine. Don't scratch my head off… you devious cat." I use the *Lyft* app and put the destination for her house. It leaves 3 minutes for small talk, so I say, "Clare. I got you a ride home. I won't be joining. Don't worry about me. I am going to be just fine."

She frowns, "Thanks. You better not drive home! I lowkey still can't stand you! I'm sure you have family that likes you. OMG, I think I'm going to be sick…"

I catch her before she falls. I sit her down, fan her and say, "Yeah, two brothers and two sisters. There is your ride." I walk her to the cab, she hesitates, thanks me again and open the car door. I close the door when her legs are in and tell her to have a safe night. Then I watch the car take off. I walk back into the bar to get a water. I check the app to make sure he is getting her home safe. After 20 minutes, I get in my car and head home to shower. That went better than I expected. Phase one is done. Can't wait til' I see her again.

On the ride home, I listen to some music. It takes 15 minutes to get to the Bronx. My little two-bedroom apartment is missing a lady. I hate that so many people drive. Finding parking is a nightmare.

After 10 minutes I can park, and I head on up to my bed. I strip off my clothes and lay down naked. Just as I'm about to fantasize about Clare, my phone buzzes. I grab it and it's none other than she.

Clare writes,

I'm home. Thank you for a fab afternoon. No more creepin up on me!

I crack up at that last one. Sweet face has no idea what she's in for. I text back,

Happy to hear that. See you soon! Get you some rest.

I close the phone and toss it somewhere. I'll find it in the morning. Might even call off work. I get up and open my first drawer. It has Clare's panties in a Ziploc. I sniff it and her scent is still there. I lay back on the bed and picture her lying next to me. The rest of my night is going to either make me happy or make me angry. My thoughts consume me on my way to sleep. I came so close tonight. Should have closed the deal. Fuck! Nothing worse than wanting what I can't have.

*****

Just as I'm about to doze off, the phone buzzes from the floor. I have to get up and find it now. The phone only went by my closet. I grab it

143

and see Clare.

There's a text.

My home, Now.

I sit on the bed, wondering if this is a drunk text. I am sure she meant to text Jackson, after all he is her man. While I shouldn't, I get dressed to head right back outside. The only thing that will stop me is if Jackson shows up because her drunken mind texted us both by accident. As soon as I'm in my car, I am flying to her house.

When I get there, the cab driver is sitting with her. He noticed she didn't look too good and knew she texted someone, so he waited. He said he was going to use her key to help her inside but didn't want to frighten her or have harassment issues in the morning. I thank him, tip him, and send him on his way.

Once he has pulled off, I use my spare key to help Clare into her apartment, undressing her once I lock the door. She's giggling and holding on to me weakly. This is my chance, so I lay her down on her bed and admire her nakedness. I close the curtains and look at her.

She's moaning, still in a drunken haze state. The drugs have set in and has hit hard since she is a newbie. She probably thinks I'm...*HIM*. Ugh. I don't strip off my clothes. Instead, I lick her nipples then ease my way to her clit. I look up at her and she is drooling.

She bites her lip and mumbles. The words are unclear, yet I don't stop. I devour her, taking in all her juices, watching as her body responds with quick sensation.

40 minutes later, I leave ibuprofen and a tall glass of water by her bedside. I wipe my mouth and smirk. Gently put her top on before exiting, no one likes waking up chilly.

Quickly exit her apartment and go home. Now I can have great dreams tonight. *Hmmm, sweet tasting, fun, gorgeous Clare.*

Chapter Seventeen

CLARE

The cab ride home feels faster than usual even though I'm across town from work. I feel horny and ready to tear a man up and down. The night was worth it. It would be my luck if Jackson tracks me using the locator. He's probably worried sick.

The cab driver asks me if I'm okay. He says I'm sweating and look pale. I blink and groggily say yes, I'm okay. I pull out my phone to text Jackson (or so I think) My home. Now. I laugh out loud.

When the driver gets to my house, he stops the engine and gets out. Suddenly the night gets fuzzy as soon as I get out the cab....
I don't feel too good!

*****

I wake up feeling dehydrated, my breath smells like vomit and too much whiskey. *That's the last time I'm going to a whiskey bar.* There's a glass of water and ibuprofen on my nightstand. I don't have any recollection of putting it there before bed. However, I take the pills and guzzle the water. I put my shorts on and grab my robe. *Weird...I only had my top on.* After getting in the cab that Tyler called, the events after are fuzzy. I cannot remember how I got in my bed, half undressed, anything.

As I walk to the kitchen to make breakfast and grab some more water, I check my phone to see who I texted last. Walking down the hall, I halt when I see the text that was meant for Jackson, was sent to none other than Tyler. I start shaking nervously, panicking. I'm such an idiot! No wonder I didn't wake up to Jackson sleeping next to me or making me hangover food.

I slide down to the floor, thinking of my next move. Today's Saturday and Thank goodness it's my day off. But shit. What to do in this moment!? Maybe I should text them both. Stressed, I put my face in my hands, groan, and get up. Headed to take a quick shower and brush my teeth, I think about what happened. My stomach growls. In the shower, I keep shifting between random moments with Tyler. It is still a blackout, I only remember laughing, more drinking, and texting Kayla. I wash up then sit in the water for 5 more minutes. I dry off, put my pj's on then put on my robe.

I need food. Now! I see that I texted Kayla as well. After I drink some water and make pancakes with bacon, she's the first one I text.

Hey girl, I'm off today. Meet me at my house so we can have girl chat. Come alone! Don't need them other bitches in my business.

I put the phone down and start a pot of coffee. I look in the cabinet to find that I'm out of roast. Now I have to go to *Starbucks* to not only buy a cup to start my day, but also buy some Blonde, Dark and Pike roast for my house.

There's one in walking distance, 10 minutes away. I change out of my pj's and toss on a yellow summer dress with white TOMS, sockless. I grab my white shoulder mini bag and put my wallet, keys, and lip gloss inside. I start to head out and call Jackson. He doesn't pick up. I lock the door and start my journey. While I'm waiting at the stop light, I use my keypad to type *Tyler*. I hesitate to call him as the countdown for the switch in the light goes down, telling me I won't be able to cross soon. I hit call as I make it across the street. Of course, he picks up.

"Shouldn't you be working?" I say.

"Should I? It's Saturday. I don't love my job the way Jackson does. I requested weekends off. You're calling me early-" he says.

I interrupt his rant to get straight to the point. "Well, I don't know your schedule. Anyways, I'm calling because I just seen the text, I sent to you. Uh, are you able to tell me what happened? Did you come over? And don't lie!!"

"Whoa. Whoa. Calm down. I didn't respond. I came home and took a shower. Why you ask?"

"Well, I woke up practically naked, with water and pain meds next to my bed...just don't know how. But if it wasn't Jackson...and it, wasn't you, then maybe the cab driver helped me open my door to get in? But Thanks for clarifying! I won't disturb your day any further." I feel like I'm rambling for no reason. A few more blocks and I can get some coffee.

Tyler laughs. "Happy to help. Don't stress it. Just be thankful that you are alive and well sweet face. Look I gotta go, I need another nap. Talk soon...or see you soon I should say?"

"Okay. You're right. You have a way with words, like a therapist. Yeah, see you when I need a cab!" I laugh and we say bye before hanging up.

I am finally in front of *Starbucks.* I walk inside and wait online. I am going to order a Venti Iced Vanilla Latte. Once I order, I wait. My phone vibrates.

Buzz Buzz Buzz Buzz

I take it out of my bag, it's Kayla.

Hey girl! I'm outside your door, where are you?

I text her my location. She asks me to get back in line and get her a Grande caramel latte and a sugar cookie. I growl, seeing as though I just got offline. But she's picking me up, so I don't have to walk back home.

They call my name for my drink after I pay for Kayla's. She walks in and traps me in a hug from behind. I tell her. "Thanks for meeting me, but I am not gonna spread my business in this coffee shop. Let's go."

She laughs, grabs my hand, and says, "let's go girl!" We both head to her car so we can gossip safely in the walls of my home.

When we get back to my apartment, she sits down on my couch. I walk over to sit next to her, and we immediately get into it. I explain the details of last night.

She's just shocked as I am. We sip on our coffees and chuckle at the nonsense.

She says, "I can't believe you went out with Tyler. Are you crazy?! What if Jackson finds out?"

I sigh. "I know. But it felt good. And I didn't tell you this one thing..."

"Spill it bitch!" She says as she stuffs the sugar cookie in her mouth.

"Okay, okay. So, my drunk ass knows for sure that I kissed him. Weird how I remember that but not anything when I got home."

Kayla is staring at me. I can tell she's secretly choking me for possibly ruining things for Jackson and me. She doesn't comment on that, instead she says "That kiss must have been good, whiskey and all. Guuurrllll, how did your drunk ass get in the house? You sound like you was drugged."

"This morning it felt that way too." I begin to wash the dishes.

"So, what does this mean girl? Are you going to ask for forgiveness and work things out with Jackson? Or try this dangerous hand with Tyler?"

I look at Kayla and say, "I have no idea. I miss Jackson, I do. But last night was the most fun I've had in a long time. Plus, I'm horny as hell-"

She interrupts me, "Uh hello, just call Jackson! And this time make sure it's him. So don't be drunk when you call bitch," Kayla laughs.

I throw the drying towel at her. "Shut up! I know that was so dumb last night. I just might call him later. Well, I did before you came but he didn't answer."

"Do you...think Tyler was *in here* last night?" Kayla starts looking around. She even walks to my bedroom.

I toss the towel down and follow behind her. I shout, "Wait Kayla. Stop. I spoke to Tyler-"

She's in my bedroom snooping now. She is determined and says, "No traces. Damn. Either he's really good or he's reeaallll good."

"Girl bye. He told me he didn't come in last night."

"And you believe him?" She says.

"Yeah girl. I told you I don't have all the details, but I have no choice but to believe him. He put me in the cab last night, not like he drove me himself."

She says, "Okay girl. Finish up. We'll leave it at that for now. I'm ready to go outside and enjoy the sun! You look cute by the way for someone to just go get coffee. Who were you tryna impress? The barista?"

Kayla is so crazy. We are back in the kitchen,

and I wrap up drying dishes. "LOL Kayla. You're very fuckin' funny. Let me fix my messy bun then we can go.

In the bathroom, I check my texts to see Jackson wrote:

Just woke up baby. Can we talk today?
I respond,

Only if you come over tonight. Be here by 8pm. Right now, I'm chillin' with Kayla.

It's only 11am. I'm giving her my day and hopefully Jackson will have my night. I fix my hair and splash water on my face.

I stare at my own reflection and give myself a pep talk. *Clare! Get your life together! Make sure you get some tonight.* I walk back out to Kayla before she knocks on the door to see if I'm alive or not. I say, "Ready to go?"

Kayla says, "Thought you'd never ask. Let's start with Central Park, I'll drive."

"Alright let's go then."

Chapter Eighteen

JACKSON

Clare is doing some shady shit or ignoring me on purpose. I called her and texted her. She didn't respond to my calls, but texted she was working late.

I'm sitting outside Q crib, wondering if she is playing me for a fool. When I went to her house, it felt strange. However, I'm not about to stay stuck on that too long, I'm gonna smoke me a blunt and chill wit Q and tell him and the boys the news.

Just as I'm about to leave my car Q calls me. "Bro, I'm outside. Come open this damn door."

He laughs and says "Aight good. I'm coming right now."

He lets me in, and he renovated since the last time we were here. His brownstone has a more classy, masculine atmosphere. The walls that were once white are now navy blue. His couch is a smooth gray. There is a glass coffee table separating the couch from the 90-inch flat screen SONY TV. I'm walking toward the kitchen with its granite countertops, and black appliances. He even has the double stove shit we used to only see in movies. The smell of chocolate chip cookies radiates from the oven. A quick sniff and I'm ready to eat a couple.

I tell Q, "Yo. I like what you did with the place my man. This shit is dope."

He is sitting on the couch, playing *Call of Duty*. "Thanks playboy! I had to switch it up for me and my honeys."

Q is such a trip. I grab a shot glass and the *Jack Daniels* bottle. I pour a double shot and think about Clare. After chillin' wit' the homies I think imma pull up. She should be home by then. She rarely stays over at Kayla's house or the other three. I wonder if Calli still feeling Q. She seen his pic once and asked Clare for a double date. I never got involved, but maybe I should so he can stop being the playboy he makes me out to be.

"Yo Jack! Come hop on the game with me! Bring the bottle wit' you. After this team match up, we are gonna call Mark and Sal."

"Bet. You better not die yo. I assume ya ass been practicing." 20 minutes later I text them.

Mark writes, *I'll pick up Sal. See you guys in few homie.*

Q says, "Aight while we wait for these clowns, tell me wassup witchu'."

I sigh. This time I grab a coke to mix with the whiskey. I sit down on the couch and tell him, "Well I got this promotion at work. I'm gonna be a chairman bro. Shit feels good. I worked so hard for this. It just proves I'm capable of opening my own company one day."

Q stands up and claps. He says, "My guy! That's wassup. You gon' make a nigga cry." He laughs. "Real talk, that's dope. How does your lady feel about it?"

I frown. "She's not answering me. She texted me saying she couldn't talk, she was busy. I'm gonna roll back up to her crib later." I take a sip of my drink. "Q, you so stupid though. Mad dramatic! I fucks with you though. What's new in your life?"

Q tells me he is still playing the field. He uses protection but starting to want a commitment. He hasn't dated since his high school sweetheart, Shanice, left him because she wanted a rich man. He wished her well and stayed to himself, focusing on his career. He currently owns his own bar on 23rd avenue.

We all worked hard to get to where we at. I hang with nothing but bosses. Mark owns his own barbershop and Sal just directed a script that's going into production for to be a movie.

I ask, "Do you have anyone in mind? You know,

to wife up. Don't forget you did what's best for you bro. Look at you now, a bossman. Love is nothing but a distraction."

The bell rings. He says, "Hold that thought. Gotta let these two in." We both walk to the door and give Mark and Sal some dap. They walk in and admire the place. Mark says, "Quentin, you really outdone yourself homie. I'm fuckin' impressed. Let me go fix up my pad too." He chuckles, whole upper chest moving up and down.

We all join in the laughter. I pat Mark on the back, "if you like his place, wait til you see mine."

"Pause bro. I'm not tryna be Clare's replacement," Mark jokes.

I slap him over his head. We all head to the couch to sit. I say, "Q was just telling me how he's ready for love. Listen up fellas."

Q says, "Damn Jackson. I just want a wife that's all. Don't make me out to be no softy."

Sal laughs. I tell Q, "Well we could help you out. Set you up. Maybe Clare knows someone that's available."

"Nobody wanna date her crazy ass friends," Q blurted.

Mark is laughing way too hard. He says, "Aight. Aight. Shots y'all." He hands out vodka shots.

I say, "Mark and Sal, I told Q already but ya boy got promoted to chairman."

They say, "**Congrats!!**" And give me a hug. Tonight is going to be another night I wake up with a hangover tomorrow. I can tell.

Q is handing out the cookies that were cooling off by the stove. We each eat one when he says, "By the way, there's weed in this shit. Enjoy!" He hands us all PlayStation 4 controllers.

We curse out the online players, smoke, and drink for the rest of the night. We joke on each other's jobs and talk about the women in our lives.

By 1 A.M. Sal, Mark and I leave. We tell Q we will catch up with him later. I'm about to see Clare.

He asks, "Are you sure about this man?"

I say, "Yeah man. I'm tryna keep my girl, not run her off into the arms of a new man."

He says, "Aight. Call me if you need me."

"Bet." We give each other a dap and a hug before I close the door.

Once I'm in the car, I start to text her but decide to just pop up. I tell Mark who's driving to drop me off at her place. I hope she's awake because I'm about to do some things to her.

Unfortunately, I had no access to get in her apartment as the locks were changed. I start shouting her name and dial her number. Nothing. After 15 minutes, I give up. I head

163

home and curse myself for all that is happening between us. She didn't seem that furious with me to up and change the locks without telling me. We been sexting here and there lately. It's confusing, but no doubt imma figure this out.

*****

This morning I woke up, took a shower, and missed a call from Clare. I was going to call her back, but I chose to check on work first.

It's 10am and I am working remotely, checking emails and making business calls. I'm drinking my coffee from my Nespresso machine. The lines and emails have paused for a minute, so I sip and think about last night. She ignored my calls, locks were changed. *Did she move on? Am I just on the sideline?* All these thoughts invade my mind.

I walk away from work for a minute and pace my house. Inhaling and exhaling, trying not to get angry. There's an instinct, just can't place it.

164

Something is off. I sit on the couch and open the compartment that hides my instant small bottle of Henney. I add it to the coffee. Time passes, and I text her. We need to talk. She tells me I can see her tonight. I'm all hype and ready to go now.

I decide to close the laptop. I text Dean to let him know to call me if he needs me. I'm tired as shit and need a nap. It's the weekend, I should be resting and not obsessing over work. I have to call Tyler later too. Need to invite him over to chill with the boys soon.

*****

I been sleep for 4 hours. For lunch, I order *Checkers*. When it arrives, I tip the delivery guy and sit down in front of the TV. I flip to TruTv to find *Impractical Jokers* is on. I eat and laugh at my favorite 4 guys. In a way they remind me of my crew.

Buzz Buzz Buzz Buzz Buzz Buzz

I reach for my phone on the coffee table. It's

Q calling.

"Wassup homie?"

"You good?"

"Yeah, I'm iight. Sitting watching *Impractical Jokers* and shit. What about you?"

"I'm doing the same shit. I wanted to see if you saw Clare last night. Did you tell her?"

"Nah man. Her locks are changed. She didn't pick up or hear me shouting. So, I dipped out. But she responded to my text asking to see her today."

"Aw shit. Don't go thinking the worst man. We know how you get. Karma ain't after you yet. Just go see her tonight, tear that ass up and be back to normal by tomorrow."

I laugh. "Quentin. You a real ass, you know that?. I don't think it's that easy, no matter how long we been together. I am happy as shit to see her though."

"Aight. Aight. Enough of the sap shit. Was just checkin' on you. Hit me up later. I'm bout to see about the new, nice, fine ass neighbor and if she has some free time for Q. Gotta let one more good one out before I become like...you."

"Yeah whatever. Hang up nigga. Peace."

Q laughs. "Fuckin' witchu' man. Peace."

Tyler is calling me soon as I end the call with Q.

I say, "Just in time. What's going on T?"

He says, "Did I call at a bad time? Why you sound so happy?"

"Oh nuttin', playa. Just got some good news, is all. But uh I wanted to ask you something."

"Shoot."

"You free to get initiated by my crew next weekend?"

I hear him laughing. "Sure, why not. Text me when and where. Say… Jackson how are things on the new position side for work?"

I pause. "It feels good, man. Real talk. I'm still a team player, so don't be ashamed to run ideas by me. I still believe in your potential. How do you do this and pick up strangers like it's nothing bro?"

"Motivation and lack of sleep homie. Aight, I see you at work tomorrow you hear? Imma enjoy the rest of my day," he says.

"BET." We both hang up.

I watch a few more episodes then turn the TV off. I use the bathroom, shower, spray this new cologne I got called *Tom Ford Noroli Portofino.*

I feel like Usher in his video when he slides across the floor in his robe. I'm feeling good about seeing Clare. In fact, I'll even make dinner tonight and pick up wine.

It's getting closer to 8pm, as it is only 6. I pick up the groceries, New York strip steaks, broccoli, and mashed potatoes. Then I go to the liquor store and grab their best wine. To kill some time, I head to the flower shop and get roses that says "I'm sorry babe. Please forgive me." It's a lavender and pink bouquet with fresh green vines.

There's nothing left to do but head to Clare. I'll be 30 minutes early; hope she is home. We have a lot to talk about. The music is playing, the night is about to feel right. I'm on a roll to get my girl back.

Chapter Nineteen

TYLER

I wake up at 10am, starving. I could cook but instead I get up, get dressed, wash my face, and brush my teeth to be on my way to walk to the bodega. I order a bacon, egg, and cheese on a roll with ketchup and mayo and grab a Fruit Punch Gatorade from the fridge. When I'm ready to pay, I slide a *Snickers* bar on the counter.

On the way back home, I chuckle as I recollect last night's encounter with Clare. If anyone had seen me, I'd for sure be busted. I assume the cab driver thought I was her man as he made no questions toward me having her key and following her inside. When I laid her on her bed and released her sexy body, I just had to taste. Now that I know her scent beyond the panties, I need more.

I arrive back home, demolish the sandwich as I was starving and keep replaying conversations between Clare and me. Her sweet laugh, and that blissful kiss. I bite my lip in response. It makes my dick hard. I take a sip of the Gatorade then toss the remains in the trash. I sit on my couch and take in the day. Suddenly my phone is ringing. I gave her a special ringtone, so I know it's her calling, "Butter Love" by Next.

She asks me if I was at her house last night. At first, I thought she had a camera in her room. I play it off and tell her to be cool, that I hadn't been upstairs. She relaxes once she hears my tone, her reaction is a little tense as if she doesn't fully believe me.

She says, "Well, I woke up practically naked, with water and pain meds next to my bed...just don't know how...." my mind trails to her naked body. I check back into the convo when she is thanking me for clearing it up.

However, I never leave empty handed. Of course, I pocketed those panties as well. They smelled like fresh jasmine and vanilla mixed with cum. As if our teasing at the bar had pleased her. Soon enough I'll have a collection by Clare and will know her every move, her schedule, sleep habits and more. There's no telling what will happen next.

After we end the call, I turn the tv on and flip the channel to college football. I am thinking about going for a bike ride today. This should be fun. Saturday nights are the ringer for easy cash as a rideshare driver, so I'll do that later.

After an hour of watching Ohio State V.S. NYU, I turn it off and gear up. As soon as I'm about to walk downstairs to the basement, there's a knock on my door.

"One second!" I yell as I tie my sneakers.

I walk to the door and grab the door handle, prepared to open it.

She smiles. She only comes to town when she thinks things aren't good.

Mom.

"Aren't you going to let me in?" She asks.

I scan myself, hinting I was about to leave for a bike ride, but she doesn't care. She pushes past me to sit on the couch. I low growl and close the door.

"Mother. Hello. What brought you here?"

"Can't a mother visit her son?"

Not you. You always need something. "Uh, sure. I just wasn't expecting you."

"I'm fine dear, thanks for asking. I'll be quick since you look like you have plans. Come sit down baby."

I brush my hands across my beard. Sitting next to Lucy, I ask, "Is everything okay?"

"Yes hun. I wanted you to know that your father has died. I need help with his funeral plans and wanted to know if I can stay with you for a while. I hate being in that big house alone."

I can't breathe. The only man that pushed me to be who I am, has fallen...for good. I jerk up off the couch and head for the liquor cabinet to take a shot of vodka. "Sure mom, whatever you need. If you don't mind, I'll be right back."

I grab my helmet from the counter and exit. I'm going to ride the bike all the way to Central Park now, to clear my head. The air is crisp, with the slight breeze grazing my skin. The sun is beaming, giving the atmosphere just the right touch to the news my mom just told me. She couldn't have told me this on the phone? I hate when she sees me break down. I'm supposed to be strong, her big boy. My dad always told me to express toughness, never shed a tear. But he is gone now, and I'm torn apart.

I stifle crying and unlock my bike. I put on Jay-Z through my iPhone headphones and hop on the bike. I swing my leg over to balance and start pedaling. While I'm riding, so many thoughts cloud my mind. The time my father showed me how to play basketball. The time I was the ring man for their vow renewal. How he tried to tell me about the morals of being a man and how to treat a lady.

Well, he wouldn't like what I'm doing to Clare. I have to call her later and tell her this. We're sort of friends now. I speed through the traffic lights, live life on the edge. After 5 miles, I slow down at a yellow light and turn the corner. I put my leg down to stop and get off the bike. I sit down on the corner to gather my thoughts. There's an angelic voice reaching closer and closer. She's singing an old school classic. The sun rays have me squinting my eyes, soon as I stand up, I bump into her.

"Oh shit. I'm so sorry," I say, holding her arm to pick her up.

She's on roller skates. She takes out one earphone to reach her hand out for a handshake.

"Oh! It's no problem! I should be more careful. I'm Calli..."

"Calli...as in Clare's, Calli?"

"Omg. How did you know? Wait a minute, are you-"

"Tyler..." I interrupt her. I give her my charming smile.

Calli starts blushing. She puts her hands in her pocket. I look her up and down. She has on a pink and purple Nike short set. Her hair is in a messy bun, and she smells like shea butter.

I put my hand in hers, extending the hold. "Nice to meet you, also sorry about the fall."

She brushes me off. "You looked kind of down, sitting on the corner. Everything okay?"

I sigh. She lucky she is cute. "I have been better. Are you hungry? There's a pizzeria down the block."

She looks me up and down. Staring at the bulge in my shorts. "Sure. I can eat." She bites her lip.

I walk my bike and she start rolling on her skates. I brief her on my dad dying. She shows compassion, giving me a hug. Her embrace is long, like she expects something after. In the pizzeria, we order 4 slices. She cheers me up with silly banter. I hadn't expected to run into Clare's friend and actually enjoy her. On the last slice she confesses.

"Tyler. I know you know who I am. I left a voicemail on your phone. Clare had your number in her bag, and I took it since she's taken and I'm not. This...can't be an accident..." She pauses, sips her root beer with a straw, eyeing me seductively. "I don't beat around the bush. You're fuckin hot. If you need some pussy, give me a call." She winks. She stands up and tosses ten dollars on the table.

"Alright. It's good to see your fine ass in

person. Wasn't sure by the voicemail if you'd be worth my while. Hey thanks, but I don't need your money sweet face."

"Keep it, so you know that I hold my own. Call me. Gotta go!" She blows a kiss as she rolls out the restaurant and just like that she is gone.

Very impressionable, I must say.

I smile, catch her kiss midair. I finish up my Vanilla coke and continue my route to Central Park. For a while, it felt as if the news of my father was a thing of the past. It felt good to laugh.

My music is playing; I'm feeling good and that's when my mom calls. I press the button to answer. "Mom, I'm good. I told you not to worry."

"Baby, should I make you dinner? What do you want so I can go to the market and get it for you?"

"Whatever you want to cook mom. I rarely have time to cook as I been busy with work." *And Clare.*

"Okay. Be safe baby. We will catch up when you get back. I love you."

"I love you too mom."

I enter Central Park West and keep riding. I hear two girls giggling. One voice, I know all too well. Their backs are turned so they can't see me. Clare and her friend are here. I think that's her day one, Kayla. I remember from her talking about her. I hide behind a tree and listen in. They just gave me my trail. I have to make it as if I'm chillin', so people don't bother me. I pull my phone out, park up the bike and slide down to the ground near the tree.

After hearing bits and pieces, of their workday and Clare's night, I ride away. I ride far enough to text her yet see how fast she responds.

Hey Clare. Miss you. We should go out again

179

soon. Anyways, I could use the drink because my mom showed up to my crib and told me that my dad died. No, I'm not looking for sympathy. Just, a friend. I don't have many of those.

She's talking to Kayla and grabs her phone as soon as it chirped. She looks at her phone and closes it. I'm a little upset but figure she don't want her friend to read it with her. I ride away and put my earbuds back in, enjoying the view. I'll give her 30 minutes before I send a follow up text.

Calli comes back to my mind and I am wondering if I should entertain the thought, put friends against each other or let it go. Calli is hot, single, and ready to do more than mingle. Her first impression has got to me.

There is the lake approaching so I slow my bike down and stop. I pull out the kickstand with my feet and sit down. My father meant a lot to me, even more to my mom. He worked his ass off to make sure we had everything. My younger brother David has his happy life with four children and his Hispanic wife. Me, I got lucky by having two jobs.

Love hasn't been something I experienced much. Love may have been in my home, but for women, I enjoy the euphoric connection of sex. It gives me energy, the chase, the excitement. It also has no attachments.

A tear escapes my eyes. I wipe my face before anyone sees. I can't be weak in public. I fold my arms in my legs and rest my head in between. Thoughts of Clare. Calli. Work. Home. My mind is quiet when a hand touches my shoulder.

She says, "Hey there. Need some wine?"

I tense up. At first, I thought it was Clare, but when she started talking, I became relieved. I lift my head and look at the body and face the hand is attached to.

She's a gorgeous, blonde hair, blue eyed,

slim, sexy lady with a crop top and jeans on. She gives the eye contact to sit, and I okay it.

"Uh, sure. Why not."

"Sorry, I'm not a creep. My name is Janice."

"Nice to meet you, beautiful. I'm Tyler."

This is going to be interesting.

*****

Janice turned out to be surprisingly nice. I guess I have good karma after all. We shared some laughs and she told me stories about her parents passing. It made me feel a little bit better. The wine was strong as hell, I think the label said *Taylor Port*. She smelled so desirable, I just wanted to lick her and fuck her right in the park. I had to maintain my composure, plus she was drunk. My first impression must always appeal to be the best.

She gave me her number before taking off. She said she had to meet up with her bestie. Girls and their commitments to each other! She hugged me before leaving and I inhaled every part of her throat. I swallowed back saliva and held on to my stiffy.

She left 10 minutes ago and here I stay trying to figure out my next move. I suppose I could text Clare and see if she wants to ease the pulsing in my penis. I get off the ground, grab the handles of my bike and flashback to Clare in the house, drunk and naked. I shake my head out of the reverie because it isn't helping me now. I text her,

Clare. I must see you. When can I see you again?

Then I hop on my bike to stop at Nick's health shop by Clare's job. I need a protein shake.

My mom texts me. Her ringer is going off in my pocket. It's nonstop and annoying. No matter how old I am, she is always blowing me up to make sure I'm okay. I don't reply back until

183

I get to the shop. I hit her with a quick, I'll be right home, do you need anything? What's the 9-1-1? Then I walk into the shop. Nick is working and is eyeing me already.

Nick's preppy voice asks what he can get me. I ask for a Banana Protein shake. My phone buzzes again, my mom wrote Nothing baby. Just making sure you're okay after I told you the news.

I tell him to give me a Strawberry Banana Smoothie as well. Nick says, "This one's on the house sexy." He reaches his hand out for my card. I uncomfortably dig in my pocket, take out my wallet and hand it to him. He winks and I can't help but laugh. He swipes the card across his payment screen and hands me my receipt. As I walk out, he says "Tell Clare I said come see me!"

I freeze. I turn my head and say, "Uh, yeah. Will do dude." I walk out, wondering how he know that I know her. Either she's been talking, or he has been stalking. I check my phone to see if she read my text, but she hasn't yet. I put the drinks in the drink hoops and in hop back on my bike. I press play on my music and let it shuffle to 90's music as I head home.

At home, mom is watching tv. She pauses it, just to greet me. I hand her the smoothie and told her Nick gave it to me for free. He was hitting on me. She laughs. She says thank you and sits back down. I walk over to the kitchen counter and call Clare again. It goes to voicemail. I curse under my breath.

My mom says, "what's wrong dear?"

I say, "Oh, it's nothing. I had a work question; my co-worker isn't answering. That's all."

"Okay Tyler. Try not to stress yourself out. Come watch a movie with me."

"In a minute, ma." I drink some of my shake and text Clare.

Clare, if you do not answer me, I'm stopping

185

by!

That should get her to respond. I look at Janice's number, ponder texting her too. It couldn't hurt to add her to my list of beautiful ladies to fool around with. I'll juggle Calli and Janice as I pull on the heartstrings of Clare. Just as I'm about to text Janice, my mom yells, "Ty! Look! *Freddy VS Jason* is on TV. Come on now, you know your daddy loved this movie." Shit. I close my phone, leaving Janice's text bubble open. I'll get back to it later.

Chapter Twenty

CLARE

The fresh air and the aroma of trees, people enjoying the sun and their families or friends all makes Central Park one of the best places to be. My favorite side is the South side, I like the ice rink and will ice skate during the wintertime.

Kayla and I are on the West side just taking a trail and talking.

"So what's been going on with you girl?" I ask her as we are passing by cyclists.

"Nothing too heavy. Real estate work is busy busy. Sometimes I wish I could just get rich while lying in my bed. Then there's this hottie that I just helped purchase a 5-bedroom home. He says he is single and preparing for the future. I can tell he wants me girl!" She laughs.

Kayla is hilarious. She's always been selective with whom she dates. She only had 3 boyfriends and we are now 28. Lucky for her, she put her career first. When her ex-Lance left her for some girl, he met in college she was heartbroken. To hear that she met someone is great news! Out of the 4 of us, only Abby and I are taken.

I look at her as we walk, "Girl. Is he tall, dark, and handsome? I hope you got his number! It wouldn't hurt to go on a date. You're a gem and my best friend. I'd date you if I were a lesbian." I pull her in for a hug.

"Thanks doll. You're not so bad yourself. Any updates with the men in your life? Has Calli texted Tyler yet?"

Now I'm laughing. I forgot Calli took his number. There's a twang feeling in my chest. It feels a lot like jealousy. "Um. I wouldn't know about that; he keeps certain things to himself. When we were out, he was focused on me." I acutely put my head on my shoulder and shrug. "Jackson is coming over tonight."

"Having your cake and eating it too. I like!!"
Kayla jokes.

"Maybe we can double date!" I say.

"Sure, pick one and let me know the time,
and place. We can even go dress shopping!"

"Now girl, you know my date will be Jackson,
stop playin'" I nudge her arm.

We spend the last of our 2-hour walk talking
about everything from people sitting on the
benches, the calm of the water, and crazy
customers. My phone chimes and it's Abby
calling. She asks how we are and what are we up
to. Kayla takes my phone and suggests another
girls night. This time the location is at my house.
I told everyone to bring food or liquor, no one
shows up empty handed, and we set it up for next
week.

Kayla and I stop at *Dunkin Donuts,* and I get a
glazed donut, grilled cheese and a medium Peach
Iced Tea. She gets hash browns and an iced Chai.

We retrieve our orders and head back to my home. She's going to help me get ready for my date!

*****

I try on several different dresses from purple to pink to red and black. Kayla made me change out of everything until I was sitting in my bra and panties telling her to "hurry up!" I was getting chilly and tired, changing in and out of clothes is not fun. Finally, she told me to wear the red.

She said, "It is like an alarm. It's sexy. You want him to say goddamn Clare, I want you back...even though you guys aren't really broken up. Oh, and change your set underneath to match. Thanks boo. This was fun." She blows on her hot pink nails and winks at me, feeling good about her decision.

She's talking about my pink bra and panties set. I tossed on hipster undies just to go outside earlier and now it doesn't match her choice. She better be washing my clothes after this!

190

"Thanks bitch! Maybe you should be a fashion designer as a side hustle," I say sarcastically.

She stands up, does a little twirl. "What can I say? I'm a woman of many talents." She gives me a hug. Then she shoos me away to go shower and get ready. "I'll leave you too it honey boo, let me know how it goes! Ooooouuu I'm so excited for you! Okay, okay. Let me get out of here. I love you girl."

All I can do is shake my head. That's my girl. "I love you too girl. Thank you so much for today. I'll call all of you later. Now go." I push her towards the bedroom door. I lay out my full outfit and go in the closet to get my red bottoms. Hopefully it'll be worth wearing. I work so much; I can't remember the last time I wore heels. With Tyler, I had flats on.

I walk in the bathroom and turn on the shower. I grab my shaving kit and put it in the shower bin. I pull the Beats pill from one of the drawers to connect *Spotify*. I play the 90's playlist and the first song is from City High, "What Would You Do?"

Before I get in the shower, my phone buzzes, it's a text from Jackson. He told me to put my feet up as he is going to cook and serve wine. I frown. I wanted to leave my house.

The water is soothing, nice and hot. I am jammin' to the music, singing along, as I start to shave. Gotta keep my body cute and flawless. Also, hairless. After 30 minutes of enjoying myself, I get out. I text him to let him know I can't wait. It's time to get dressed and I spend an extra 10 minutes trying to figure out how to style my hair.

I decide to just put it in a nice clean bun. I brush my edges and apply gel to my hair, so I'm frizz free. Then I put on my MAC red lipstick. I head to the living room and pour myself a shot of *Cîroc, Red Berry*. I'm feeling this red theme.

I think about a that has happened in the past

week, waiting for Jackson to come. Just as my mind drifts to the night I got home from hanging with Tyler, my bell rings. I forgot to get a new key for Jackson...or maybe he deserves to earn it? My locks were changed, and I made no questions about it. It didn't seem necessary; I just went with the flow. I figured, it was a sign telling me that it's time for a change.

Anyways, I buzz him up using the intercom and then leave the door open. I sit with my legs crossed on the couch, waiting for him. He walks in the room and his scent eludes me. I can't quite place it, but it's new and has to be off market. Either way he smells so good.

"Hey Clare."

I smile and say, "Baby. Hello. Where have you been all this time? Love the new scent."

"You know me baby. Work and chillin'." He reaches in to give me a kiss and a long hug.

I've missed this. I inhale as he pulls away and

walks to the kitchen to place the items he brought on the counter. He says, "I'm all about you tonight. Tell me baby, what's up with you? What happened the other day, it felt like you were avoiding me."

I swallow. All of a sudden, I feel jittery. Can't let him see me sweat. I finish up my drink and grab the bottle of wine he bought. *Chateau Canon 2010*, a little young but hey!

He says, "You don't want to eat first?"

I reply, "Oh come on. Let me have a glass of wine dammit! Besides work has been busy and I been giving you your space. Give me a break Jackson! As for the door, I didn't know they were going to do that and quite frankly I didn't ask because I don't give a fuck. They just replaced my key and we kept it pushin'."

Now I'm sitting at the bar stool. I'm giving him a hard glare as he just pissed me off. I pop the bottle and pour it into a wine glass he already had on the counter.

"Well alright then. Dinner will be ready in 25 minutes. I'm not done with you yet! Let's pause this for table talk. In lighter news I had called you to tell you that they want me as chairman! How dope is your boy now?" He dusts his shoulders.

I laugh. "Congrats my love! That's huge! Sorry I missed this news. Everything has been so confusing...between us. Then I did some self-healing. Look at my dress! Trying new things. Come boo, gimme a kiss."

He walks from around the island and kisses me. It's long, passionate, and sweet. It feels as if we are stuck in time. These are the kisses that make me want to take him down right here in this kitchen. I pull away before the urges increase.

"Damn baby you've missed me *that much*," he emphasizes at the end of his statement.

"Shut up. You missed me too, I see," I draw my eyes to his girth. Very happy to see me.

Jackson turns away and says, "I always want to bend you over a counter, but first we eat."

Something about the way he said "eat," had an erotic pressure that turned my thoughts naughty.

Jackson's chiseled chest, strong muscular thighs, and them big, manly feet. His hard-working hands and those deep, pulsating...eyes. His third leg beating, begging, asking for its woman. *His* woman.

"Um. Clare. Can you hear me? Did you have too much on an empty stomach?! Babe..."

I snap out of my reverie. "Huh? Oh yeah, my bad. I'm good. How much longer until we eat?"

"10 minutes." He pours himself a glass.

We have steak, broccoli, and mashed potatoes. Yum! Can't wait to dive in. I'm starving. This food has to hurry up.

"Oh. I also got you these. He pulls out this

big, bright yellow bag that I clearly missed when he came in. He reveals the most beautiful flowers ever. There's a note, *I'm sorry baby. I acted like a fool. I Love You. Please forgive me, on your time of course.*

Tears well in my eyes as I read the card. He is so sweet. His mama raised him oh so well. I raise my arms to signal for him to come to me. "Thank you. They mean a lot to me. I'll put these in water." We embrace for the remaining of time. The timer for the stove beeped into our moment.

He makes our plates. My stomach growls. I sit at the dining room table. As he is setting the table he asks, "Soooo is Calli still single?"

I laugh. Inside, I'm wondering why. "Yeah, she's crazy. No one wanna date her ass. Why wassup?"

"Oh. Not for me baby. Calm down. I can see the look in your eyes. Was thinking about hooking her up with Q."

197

I choke on my wine. "I don't see them pairing very well. Maybe he'd be good for Sabrina. But what do I know? I'll ask her and see if she feels up for a date with him. Cool?"

"Cool." He speaks. He sits down. "Time to dig in babygirl."

We don't talk and eat. Not all the time. The way Jackson cooked this steak, has me licking my fingers and sucking the butter off my lips. He's watching me. I think I ate all my food a little too quickly. My stomach is happy and full. I sip my wine and wait for him to finish so we can go back to the conversation from earlier.

Jackson cleans up. He wet the rag and wiped the table up. He refills our glasses and sighs. Something is heavy on his chest.

"Clare. I don't know how else to express this. I don't want every time we meet up to have conflict. But where were you when you ignored me? And why don't I have a key to this new door?

What if something happens to you?!" His eyebrows furrow, he slams his hand on the table. Then he swipes his hands on his face.

I can see the pain, the hurt and the confusion on his face. I have to approach this in a manner that shuts this shit down now. "Jackson. First off-- calm down! Ok? It's not what it seems. I had a few drinks the other day with friends, and I just TOLD YOU the locks were changed. Sorry last time I checked, you haven't been here in months!"

I stand up now. I'm pissed. *How can he give me apology flowers then ruin our night all in one?* I walk over to the window and turn back toward him. "Jackson, you were hurt by my outlash at *Starbucks*, now you come to my home to hurt me by assuming?" Even though in a way, he is not wrong, I think as I pace back and forth.

"Clare. We are still in love. Or I am. I'm not so sure about you anymore. But you're right. I came over here to fix things. How foolish of me to think you are stepping out on me. Are you going to give me a spare key?"

He walks over to me. He wraps his arms around me, and it feels so good.

"Jackson. You have to earn the key sweetie. We still have to burn all our issues. You pulling this shit, just messed with my head."

"Clare..."

"No Jackson, I need a minute." I walk toward the bedroom. I take the time to relax. I think of texting Tyler, but that wouldn't help right now. I plop myself on the bed and instantly see stars. I rub my eyes together and get up slowly. I inhale and exhale long enough to fall into a slumber.

Jackson walks in the bedroom. "Clare. Let's talk about this please!"

I pop open my eyes. He can't be serious. This just pissed me all the way off.

Chapter Twenty-One

JACKSON

"Absolutely not!" Clare is yelling at me. I think the alcohol has her riled up. I shouldn't have approached her tonight. Now I have to tame the wild beast.

"Baby, baby. I'm sorry. I just thought since I caused the distance between us, you'd step out on me. How can I earn your love back, your trust and the key?" I walk over to her. I sit on the bed and caress her thigh.

"Jackson, you can't come up in here causing stress after the last time you had me looking crazy! In public at that! Remember you didn't know my needs. Now this?"

"Come on Clare. Don't act like you're not sexy. Any man will gladly take you away from me. You know how it is. When people ignore calls and don't see each other, that's a sign of being pushed away."

She walks by the window. Looks outside, then turns to me. I know how to fix us.

I take off my tie and release my button up, tossing it to the floor. I pull her into me. kissing her ear lobe. I whisper, "Forgive me Clare," and kiss her right cheek. She moans.

"Jackson...wait." She closes her eyes. "You're still my love. I trust you..."

She wants to play hard to get, just like how we first met, but I'm not letting her get away with it this time. "Tell me...how can I... make it up to you..." I say in between kissing her neck. She is so open right now. I lick her neck as I go lower.

Clare bolts up. "Jackson. Maybe we should finish talking. I need another drink."

She begins to trail toward the kitchen, but I grab her hand. I yank her gently backwards to me. I strip off my pants, leave my boxers. The look on her face is enough for me to continue. She bites her bottom lip and now I'm ready to go.

"Oh God, Jackson. I Want You!"

I swing her into my left arm and kiss her deeply. Then I lift her back up and use one hand to zip down her dress. The lingerie reveals itself and the red is alarming. Shit, she's beautiful! I lick my lips, making my way to her supple breasts with my eyes locked on hers. Lust is in her eyes and for damn sure in mine. I unclasp her bra and peck until there is a nipple in my mouth. Clare moans loudly. Without protest, I switch between her nipples, flickering my tongue and sucking with intensity. Clare starts grinding, so I slip my finger in her panties. Mhmm she's wet.

I groan as I slide her panties to the floor. I direct her to the bed, lay her down and get to feasting. She tastes very sweet, succulent. I can't stop, not until she's at her breaking point. The way she is moving, shows just how bad she needed this. I insert two fingers into her wetness and look up at her as she bites her lip and releases a sensational moan.

My dick is getting hard; her juices are filling my throat. I stop to fuck her, when she leans on her elbows, putting a finger to my mouth.

"Swallow it. It's my turn baby," Clare says, pulling my boxers down.

I do as I'm told.

She eases her way down and I close my eyes. I rest my head in my arms as she gives me the best head I've had in a while.

"Fuuuccckkkk baby! Slow down," I say as Clare is sucking me dry. It feels so good, I don't want to nut so fast. She's bobbing and deep throating my cock as if I'm the best dessert she's had in a long time.

I groan, loudly. She stops and jumps on top of me. Clare is taking the lead and I let her. Our bodies are speaking to each other. This feels too damn good. A little bit of the wine and distance passion, has us on a wild ride.

It's my turn, as I said I have to tame the wild beast. I flip her on her stomach and spread her legs. I slide inside her pussy and pound her real good. I grip her love handles as I go faster. She's gritting her teeth and looking back at it.

"Yes daddy. Fuck me gooooood. This is yours. Take it. Own it!" She cries out.

"You like that? Oouu yes babygirl. Imma show you what you missed." I stroke her harder, going deeper.

"Faster baby!! Fuck MEEEEE!!" She screams.

My hands guide her to perk her ass up more, so I can go deeper in doggy style. This plump, voluptuous ass of hers has me pumping hard.

Sex is so damn sexy, hot, and thrilling. I nut after an hour of showing my baby that she is mine to keep, no matter what we go through. I lay on the bed to catch my breath.

Clare climbs on top, kisses me and says,

"Shake it off boo, cuz' we goin' round two!"

Well goddamn!

She walks out the room, still naked. She comes back with two whiskey shots. We toast, make eye contact and down it. She smacks the shot glass out my hand. Clare says, "I'm ready. I'm not waiting for you." She inches down to my cock and slides it into her mouth, her tongue slithering like a snake.

I can't refuse. Instead of the twenty minutes to recharge, I only needed five. Clare's bold, freaky, take-charge moment is fuckin hot. I lead her head with my hands, the feel of her tongue and the back of her throat making me want to nut right now.

I tell her, "Honeybee...let's...ughhhh...go by the.... damn Clare...shit...Clare...go...go... buh...by... the window!" I'm speaking in tongues as she puts in that throat work. Her mouth is very wet, the strokes are getting me high, I'm pulsating in her mouth. She grips the bottom part of my shaft with both hands, motion them as she massages my balls.

She looks up at me and doesn't stop for another fifteen minutes. She swallows my precum. I touch her cheek and say, "Baby please. I'm ready to make love to you."

Finally, she gets off of me and walks to the window. She smacks her ass and says, "Come get it baby."

I crawl on all fours to Clare with my mouth open and dick swinging.

"Ooouuu" she coos.

I lick her cunt for a second time, from the back, taking in all the wetness, our scent, the fire burning in our love making. I stand up, make out with her. I slide my penis inside her pussy and slow grind while we stand. We are on the side panel by the window, and don't care who peeps. We are too in the moment to stop. I palm her ass while she grinds on top of me.

"Mmhhmmm. Fill me, Jackson. I wanna feel all of you," she says seductively.

"As you wish my lady," I say in a low baritone.

Clare decides to change the position after a couple minutes. There's a chair on the other side so she leads us to it and pushes me down. She climbs on top of me, breasts bouncing in the air, and fucks the shit out of me. Her pacing is so fast, exhilarating and I love it. I don't want this night to end. She's gyrating and grinding on me with all the pent-up tension from our distance illuminating in the room. I grip her waist, pumping her as she rocks back and forth.

"Jackkksssooonnnn. Ugh, yes. Gimme all of this dick!"

"Clare...damn girl...slow dooowwnnn...I'm about to...cum," I whisper in her ear, gripping her booty.

"Cum baby, I'm cumin' too," she says, breathlessly, mid orgasm.

After forty-five more minutes, we take a breather. I look at her and we laugh in unison. Then we get off the chair to clean ourselves up.

I smack her ass on the way to the bathroom.

"Stop playing before there's round three in the shower," she teases.

"Oh nah baby, I'm tapped out. Chill," I say, laughing. I put my arm around her, and we head to the shower. My intent wasn't to argue, as much as it was to take back what's already mine. Plus, make up sex is always better.

******

After Clare and I took a shower, I stayed an extra thirty minutes. Then I got a text from Mark,

Yo, you might wanna go home bro. Things not lookin' too good.

209

I gave Clare a kiss and told her I have to go, things sound urgent at my house. I start to dress myself, starting with the button up, my boxers and then I find my pants beside the bed. I put them on leg after leg, buckling my belt. She whines as she watches me. I say, "It's okay baby, I'll be back soon. Get a spare key so I can sneak up on you on the late night." She laughs and that's the last thing I hold on to on my way out.

I rush in my car and take off. I park and hurry home. I unlock my door and all of the crew is there. All I hear is "Surprise!"

Mark is first up and says, "Yo Jack, you forgot you agreed to celebrate my B-DAY at your house man?!"

I palm my face. "Yeah, my bad homie. I got caught up with Clare." I take my suit jacket off, hang it in the coat closet. Mark hands me a white T-shirt and my black Nike shorts to change into so I can "be comfortable in my own home," his exact words.

Q walks over to us as he sees Mark and I embrace in a hug. He says, "Thank god for your spare key! You be too busy lost in Clare sauce to remember party plans!"

I laugh. Sal pats me on my back. "Welcome home!"

I notice the weed bar, liquor station and an all you can eat buffet. I yell, "I hope y'all cleaning this shit up when it's over!"

Q says, "Relax. You know if they don't gotchu', I for sure got you! Have you asked Clare about Calli?

I say, "Thanks my man. Oh, yeah and she said she will talk to her." I walk to the bathroom to quickly change clothes. The atmosphere is filled with excited chatter, loud music, weed and dancing. We know how to throw some parties!

Q is standing by the door, and he blurts out, "Aight, bet. Now come enjoy this party man. Let's go smoke." He says, while we walk to the weed bar and grab a blunt.

I text Clare.

These clowns made it seem like someone broke in my house, just for it to be them having a party for Mark! Lol. I'll check you later though.

She writes back,

Lol your homies are something else! But they love you. Don't have too much fun.

I laugh, a stripper with a big, plump ass and a bikini thong with the matching top comes over. She starts dancing on Q. I puff on the blunt, inhale smoke. When I pass him the blunt, he passes me the stripper. I exhale as smoke escapes my lips. She starts dancing on me before I can decline. I raise my hands, shocked.

Q says, "Relax! A little lap dance won't hurt."

"Shut the fuck up and pass the joint." I look at the girl, she's hella sexy. Ciara's "Ride" comes on. The stripper grinds on me. Another girl comes and dances on Q. I look for Sal and Mark and they seem occupied by other strippers as well. Two are surrounding Mark, I hope he don't break into temptation as he has a girl at home. I focus back on shawty that's on me. I ask her, "what's your name?"

She says, "Jessica. You must be Jackson...right? I was told to wait for you."

Shocked, confused, and curious, I reply, "Oh is that so? What you got in store for me." My eyes are heavy, and I start to feel high. She goes crazy, like she's the real Ciara. My mind has dirty thoughts. I palm her ass while her back is turned to me. Then, she turns around and rocks back and forth. This...is no good. Very risky. My dick is getting hard. She smiles. I pull her to my ear, "Excuse me."

She bites her lip and gets up. There's a strong hunger look in her eyes. She walks over to Q, and I walk to the liquor station. I pour me some *Jack Daniel's Honey Whiskey*.

Jessica is a goddamn beauty. I can't get frisky after promising Clare I am all she needs. These fools know temptation is easy tonight. I have got to get everyone out before it becomes a lust party. For now, I'll enjoy the vibe. I pour another shot of whiskey and pull a chick from her friend. They were in the middle of talking. I ask if she wants to dance. She smiles and complies. After this I'm going to gather the guys for a little private conversation to ask what the fuck were they thinking!

*****

I walk over to Sal and tell him to bring Mark to the backyard. Q is still enjoying his minaj-a-trois with the girls; I step up to him and tap his shoulder. "Playboy, let's go. Backyard, now. Urgent meetin' wit the crew.

He huffs, tells the girls he will be right back, then follows me. Once we are all outside, I'm the first to speak. "Aight, first off Mark, I hope you're having a good ol' time up in here. Happy birthday!" I give him some dap. He nods and I continue, "Y'all know this is bad for me, right? I just seen my lady."

Mark laughs. Q turns away. Sal speaks, "Listen man. I didn't know where you were until I got here. I was running late. But it's a party, so what, a couple little fine honeys shouldn't break your loyalty." He smirks and smooths his hands together.

I swipe my left hand over my head. "Strippers? Okay. Random fine ladies? Come on now. Temptation is never good for nobody. Mark, you better count your days."

"Bro. No doubt. We will just have twice as many strippers for your birthday," he puts me in a knuckle sandwich.

"Yo get off me, before you get sent to the hospital for your special day," I joke. "Aight I'm done messing with y'all, let's see if I can keep it in my pants tonight."

I turn to walk back inside, when Q says, "Aye, did you fuck Clare? How was dinner?"

Mark and Sal are behind him. They are all waiting for my answer.

"Uh, yeah. Of course. She couldn't stay away from alllll of this for too long," I joke, licking my lips, gliding my hands down my chest and lift my shirt. "Besides, we had a little fight, but the sex was worth it. I dicked her down and then she rode me like a rodeo. It felt good." I bite my lip, rehashing the moment in my mind.

They look at each other and bust out laughing.

"Aight, aight. We ain't need all that. Let's go," Q says.

"So let me know which stripper you want, and I'll ease up," Mark says to me, jokingly then heads back in.

"Glad you and Clare made up man. It was

rough seeing you two fight. Y'all like mom and dad," Sal says.

These muh'fuckas, always have some slick shit to say.

I start to walk back in, then I hear my name being called when a song ends. It's coming from the front. I make my way through the party to open the door.

Q has beat me to it. In rushes Tyler. He seems pleased to be here. *I hadn't invited him, so how did he get here?*

"Tyler, what's good?" I say, we give each other a pound.

"Hey. I heard from your assistant there was a surprise party for your friend. I thought I'd come by. Is that alright with you?"

"You're already here. Sure, enjoy. Plenty of strippers to go around," I say, questioning what he said in my head.

"Where's Mark?" Tyler asks.

"Around here somewhere. I'm faded and tipsy, so help yourself," I manage to say. I close the door behind him.

Q asks, "Is he trustworthy? He can dip out now--"

I interrupt him to say, "Yeah, he's cool. We were business partners before I got promoted."

He says, "Bet. Holla if you need me. Imma get another drink and bag one of these ladies."

We give each other a five, then he leaves. I walk over to pull on a blunt. This fine young lady comes up to me with her blunt in hand, ready. I stare and observe, waiting for her next move.

She puffs. Glares at me. She says, "Yo, wanna hit?"

I can't tell if she means the weed or her body. I chance it. "I'd love to sweetie."

She hands me the blunt. Then gets all up in my personal bubble. I'm about to grip her waist, as Tyler jumps by.

"Hey man, aren't you taken?"

I grit my teeth. "What do you want Tyler!?"

"Just protecting your girl's heart. I'm a nice guy," He says.

"Oh, is that it? You want her? Take her..." I turn to the woman, "I didn't get your name, but it was nice while it lasted.

She says, "it's Charlene. Nice to meet you too." Then she turns to Tyler.

I walk away. If he's going to be trouble, he can get the hell out my house.

Chapter Twenty-Two

CLARE

I know for a fact; Jackson and I are toxic. But, sexy and toxic. We aren't bad for each other; we just make up to break up to make up again. Dinner was so good. Sex was even better. I had wished we could cuddle to sleep, but then his homie called and as always, he has to pick up and leave. They're like the second job no one asked for.

Here I am, sitting like a cheap hoe, feeling like he fucked me and dissed me. I shake off the negative thoughts and go in the cabinet in the kitchen to snack on Cheez-Itz. Now I'm bored and it is 1:50a.m. I shoot Kayla a text,

Hey girl, I got some tea for you! Call me later. K, bye.

I look through my messages and open Tyler's text. He has some news he wants to share and wants to do it over drinks. I'm not sure if that's the right thing to do, especially not after the way Jackson put it down. He reclaimed me all over again. Damn, that was hot.

I respond to Tyler, as a friend, of course.

Oh no. Anything that involves talking and drinking just can't be good. And you hinted at just friends, you could use one. But let me check my schedule and I'll get back to you.

I put the phone on the kitchen counter and go turn the TV on. I press the channel directional pad until I see something interesting. *Love and Hip Hop* is on, so I sit and watch until my eyes get heavy all over again.

****

Dinner, Sex, and TV knocked me out like a light. I wake up to my stomach growling at 9 a.m. I don't feel like cooking, so off I go to get breakfast. I wash my face, brush my teeth, and put on orange yoga bra and leggings set with my *Victoria Secret* flip flops. I snatch my wallet off the

221

dresser and my phone from the kitchen counter, before getting my keys to head out. I can't find my Sailor Moon bag, and at this point I feel too old for it.

The sun is bright, and the day feels good. I walk to the corner store. Some reason, I feel like I'm being followed. Maybe it's the recovery from the night, I need more sleep. I keep hearing people yell at someone shoving them out the way. I turn around to find a police officer running. Before I panic, I speed walk to the store.

The officer runs past me, and I drop my mini purse, everything falls out. I collect all my items then enter the store and take a breath of air. Very eerie and awkward situation, I grab a bottle of water out the fridge and yell, "Don't worry I'll pay for this," as I take a drink. Then I go to the man behind the cooking area and ask for an omelet with broccoli and cheese and a side of home fries.

While I wait, my phone chimes. It sings, "If I

Don't Have You," by Tamar Braxton. It's Jackson.
He leaves a text,

Thinking of you. Get this, these fools had a surprise party for Mark. At my house. These negros! Real talk though, I had a good ass time. You good?

I frown. Did he fuck someone else? Make out? What was so fun. I close the text before I respond with rage. My meal is ready by the time I look up. I pay for it and the water, then head on home.

I had planned to stay home, but I got a call from work as I'm busting this food down. My co-worker asks if I can go in from 11a.m to close. I growl and say sure. I need the money. I eat and start to get ready.

Just what I needed! A workday. Hopefully no drama. Kayla texts me just in time, says she can't wait to hear what's up. I ask her for a ride to work, she says she's on her way and will be here in 5 minutes.

****

On the way to work, I tell Kayla about dinner with Jackson. She has mixed emotions, one for his assumptions and another for the make-up sex.

She says, "Girl, y'all toxic, but that sex gotta be something!" She keeps her eyes on the road. Then she warns me to be careful with Tyler. I chuckle and nod my head. I look through the rearview mirror, I think I see Tyler. The car behind us resembles his model, but Kayla is driving so fast, it can't keep up. I start to panic, and scream, "drive faster!"

She's worried. She turns to look at me, quickly and speeds up. "What's wrong? What the fuck am I speeding for?"

I inhale. Swallow the saliva that's left in my mouth and say, "I think we're being followed."

She looks at me and laughs. "Oh girl! I thought it was something else. No one is stalking us girl, stop it. Now I'm gonna chill before I get pulled over."

"Okay." I slowly turn my head to see if the car is still behind us. It's not. Kayla pulls over and parks the car.

She says, "Is there something you want to tell me?"

I make sure the car isn't around. I start to speak, stuttering. "It's, uh...Tyler. Okay. Ever since he showed up to my job, that time Jackson also stopped by, I get this weird thing about him...like, like, he's following me everywhere."

Kayla is shocked and frightened. She holds my hand. "Baby girl! Why didn't you tell me? And here you are going out with him and shit. Is that so he doesn't suspect that you know? Or you like him?

I say, "No. I genuinely like him. I'm crazy. I know. I think I'm paranoid more so because I feel guilty, lying to Jackson." I smooth out the wrinkles in my pants. "Shit speaking of Jackson! I have to text him back!"

"You have to get this sorted out and fast, girl. Let Calli hook up with him. Wait, you guys didn't have sex, right?"

"No! Just friendly flirting for now. Although, I do have dreams about him."

"Ah, I see. That's why you and Jackson had sex. Gotcha'!"

"Ugh. Kayla! Shut up!" I punch her arm, playfully. "By the way, Jackson also had a surprise party for Mark last night. There were probably strippers and hoes there, you know how men are."

"True," she says, while reapplying her pink M.A.C. lipstick. "But you also know how your man is. So don't worry about that. Let's get you to work before you get sent home." She puts the car back into drive and I make it to work within 10 minutes after she pulled over.

I thought about my life as we drove past coffee shops, *Dylan's Candy Shop*, the *AMC* movie theater, and other stores that catch my eye. Before getting out, I glance at her. "Thank you for everything girl. You're the best! Love you. Text ya on break if I get one. Also, you're right, I need to give Jackson the benefit of the doubt."

She winks. That's my queue to head on in. I check my phone. Before I can walk through the glass doors to *Barnes and Noble*, a hand covers my mouth and pulls me closer to them, pulling me away from the door.

Chapter Twenty-Three

TYLER

My mom and I enjoyed the *Freddy VS Jason* movie, just like old times. However, my mind was displaced many times thinking about seeing Clare. Soon as the movie ends, I tell mommy dearest, I'll be back. She laughs because she knows I never stay still.

I take a quick drive to Clare's house since she isn't answering my call. I park across the street and get out. I stop and look directly at her window. The curtains are open, leading me to seeing what I shouldn't: Jackson fuckin' Clare. I can't take my eyes away from them, furious, then I see Clare head to the chair with his bare ass about to sit down. She starts riding Jackson.

I kick the wheel of my car. This bitch either leaves the curtains open or closes them slightly and the one chance I come by; he is here! I pace back and forth. Then she has the nerve to fuck him on a chair!? This is bullshit.

I watch. No one is outside. Perfect. When they are finished, I get back in the car and drive off before Jackson asks why I'm here. I get lost in my thoughts, no direction of what to do next. I cruise around for fifteen minutes; wouldn't it be fun to go to Jackson's house? I pop his address in the GPS and follow the "turn right onto Bedford Ave."

I park a few blocks away just in case. I drive around in a circle until I see him pull up. There's loud music coming from his house. This should be fun; I find parking and comb my hair. I spray cologne, as I know there's some ladies in there. I listen to three songs; it should give enough time for him to get settled into this party.

While I am driving, someone has their thumb out for a taxi. Never one to ignore money, I pull over. I show him my license. I told him, "I can get you there faster than you waiting on service. I do *Uber* and regular taxi. Come on, get in."

He looks at me with worry. Then he scans my license and gets inside. He says, "Thanks dude. I am just going 10 minutes away, but I am high as hell."

He tells me his address and I enter it into the GPS. Then I speed away to drop him off, so I can hurriedly get back to Jackson. I think I got him home within 6 minutes, the way I was speeding. He tipped me $10. I thanked him then went back to Jackson's house.

I knock on this door. A guy answers the door, I'm assuming he's one of his friends. I push right past him, in search of Jackson who walks right into view. He looks a little pissed off that I'm here. I ask, "Where's Mark?" And when I'm told he's around, I make myself comfortable. I only know about Mark because Jackson's assistant said he's the birthday boy. No man answers the door on their big day. Tonight's my opportunity to become one of the boys.

I see Jackson being a flirt and I interject

because I'm an asshole. He will not hurt my little Clare. No, no, no! I should just take pictures, but the route I'm taking with Clare is much more satisfying. She'll be moaning my name for real and not just dreaming about me. Jackson probably wishes I leave.

I pull out my singles and start throwing them at the strippers. The girl he was talking to, Charlene, she's a baddie. I can see why he was talking to her. I might get back to her later. When Jackson walked away, I winked at her and walked to the bar. I pour myself a shot of whiskey. Maybe if I get drunk tonight, I'll forget about what I have seen in the window.

Jackson took all the boys to the backyard to chat. I pour four shots of this *Ciroc Red Berry* and walk to meet them as they close out the meeting. As they enter back into the house, they each say, "Thank you new boy Tyler! Good looks."

Jackson, squints his eyes then laughs. "Tyler, are you stalking me? How the hell did you know we was having a party?"

"Oh, I just have my ways partner. You should watch who you work with." I pat him on the back. I add, "Don't worry. I won't cock block your night any longer. Introduce me to the team! Remember you said I can be down with the crew."

He sighs. "Alright man." One by one he introduces Q, Mark, and Sal. I mentally scan their faces, so I recognize them from now on. We all take another shot together and continue to party.

I stay for about two hours then leave. I go home to sleep naked, ready for tomorrow.

******

The sun rays wake me up and I don't want to get up. I roll over, placing the pillow over my head. Just five more minutes, I growl to myself. I drag my body off the bed, slugging as I rise to the occasion to go on over to Clare's. I get dressed, make coffee, add vanilla syrup and hazelnut creamer, heat up a hot pocket and fly out the door. Again, I park away from her home, as I did for Jackson's, so I'm not noticed. I see her leaving to go to the store. Carefully, I walk a few feet behind her, following her to the store. There's a crowd, so I am passing in between people, pushing some and zig zagging through. Clare's pace increases and I up my tempo until police push pass me and a few other people. I immediately turn into a different store to hide.

I wait a couple minutes then walk back to her house. I hide behind this tree across the street. Clare is getting in the car with Kayla. I run to my car to follow them. I stay about five cars behind, zig zagging occasionally to avoid being seen. Kayla's car speeds up and I think she knows I'm following them. I turn off and decide to beat Clare to her job. Not sure if that's where she is going, but I see her name tag go in her purse after she picked up her belongings when the police flew past her.

I arrive and wait patiently, checking the time on my watch. Clare is texting on her phone. As she shows up to the front door, I snatch her from behind, covering her mouth. I pull her into a wall and whisper, "How much longer did you plan to ignore my call, sexy?" I shush her, as I stick my finger down her pants. Clare moans. She buckles her legs, rocks back and forth. Enjoying this abrupt altercation.

I talk, voice a little high octave, deep voice protruding. "I'll let you get to work. But you will meet me tonight so I can finish what I started and tell you what I have been waiting to share over drinks." I remove my hand from her pants and put both fingers in my mouth.

I smile and walk away. It's my day off. After last night, I am glad to be on my own time. I hope Jackson's having a good day, in his happy new position. Nothing left for me to do, best to go home. At home, mommy dearest is gone. I sigh, scratch my head, and decide to text her.

Oh motherrrr, sweetie. Where have you taken off to?

I press the button on top of the phone then place it on the kitchen counter. I take a bottle of water out of the fridge and relax. I can't help but laugh at the impulsive action to please Clare before work. My thoughts lead me to my bedroom. In my drawer, I take out the *Ziploc* bag with her purple panties and sniff. Ahh, still smells like her. My mind trails to when she was fucking Jackson on the chair. I so badly wish that was me. I fantasize about her, about us. I take the panties with me to the bed, bite them as I unzip my pants.

I pull my member out and jack off with the image of Clare riding me. Once I'm done, I snicker. Maybe a little too demonic. Since my mom is staying, I have to clean up quick. Who knows when she will come back.

I take a hot shower. As the water breaks through my pores, work stuff is on my mind. I have to plan out my next moves to have the best partner so I can end up on the same level as Jackson once again. Just when I think I've got him where I want him, he's been promoted.

I hear, "Tyler baby, I'm back. I went out to see some friends." My mother returned just in the nick of time. I turn the water off, get dressed and go make conversation to kill the time. She loved my father like no other. It's a shame he was taken from us so sudden.

I ask mom, "what's your best memory of dad?"

She smiles. "Sit down Ty. I'll tell you all about it." She gets a water out the fridge, and we sit down on the couch. "Well, when he had an affair with your best friend's mother, it took all of me not to slip laxative in his meals every night."

I blink. Speechless. I hope she is joking.

"I think I need some wine," she laughs and walks over to the wine fridge.

"Ma, you not serious...are you?" I ask, holding my water bottle a little too tight.

"You think your dad was always innocent baby? Oh no. Let's talk."

Ugh, great. There's nothing like a woman scorned.

Chapter Twenty-Four

JACKSON

That was one hell of a party. All the sexy ladies had me questioning my loyalty. If Tyler hadn't blocked me so many times, I'd probably fuck someone after I just got done with Clare hours prior to that night. I'm surprised my neighbors didn't call the cops; it was so loud. Then again, I think most of them were in my house. The boys know how to rally up any and every one they see for a party. If your light is on, best believe you're getting invited. My mind is always focused on work and Clare, I don't know what my neighbors look like. Hell, I might need to host a party just for that.

Aight check it, so I'm in bed, dreading this work shit. I realized I overshared to Clare in the text. She's a jealous woman even though she sexed me so good. Surprisingly her response was...normal. She said,

Glad you had fun. Don't have too much though, you're a super prestige businessman ;).

A smile eases on my lips. Now I can start my day on a good note.

Today's suit is red plaid with a pink button up. I look in the bathroom mirror, feeling myself. "When you look good, you feel good," I say to my reflection, smoothing out my beard. I do a spin, feeling my swag. Everything seems to be going right for me. I grab my keys and stop by *Starbucks* before work to grab a bacon, egg and cheese and an Iced Grande Vanilla Latte.

Once at work, I walk to my office. I'm moving to an office upstairs, so I have lots of packing to do. I only started with a frame of Clare and me. I play some smooth R&B on the Bluetooth, continue packing and sing as the songs play. The intercom buzzes, Carrie, the new girl who will be working for Tyler, notifies me that there's a new female employee. Monica. I tell her to send her in.

Coming in, sashays this 5'4, brown skin, gorgeous caramel skinned woman...sorry...Monica...with honey brown box braids trickling down her back, which is open as her black dress accentuates her body with fiery red heels. It takes all my self-control not to jump on her right now. Damn, she's fine! I had to stop packing to admire her beauty.

She smiles. "Hello, I'm Monica. But you knew that. Jackson, right?"

I look her up and down. Then I reach my hand out for a handshake. "Yes. Nice to meet you, Monica. You're beautiful, by the way."

She blushes. "Thank you. Are you, my boss?"

"You can say that. I just got promoted. I won't be in this office, as you see, but I'll be around."

"That's too bad." She hasn't released my hand until now. Her perfume permeates the room.

I ask. "What you know about IT girl? Not

stereotyping. More impressed."

She winks. It's hot. "I graduated from MIT just three months ago. I have plans to open my own firm one day and give back to the children of the community who cannot afford an education because they lack funds for technology."

That's sexy as hell! I clap. "Wow. Super impressive. Hey I'll back down. You have a chip on your shoulder. Do you need a tour?"

"Thank you very much. It's hard being a nerd and an IT girl. I would love a tour, when you have time..." she raises her hands to the room to initiate me packing.

"Right. I will have the tour scheduled for you in about fifteen minutes. For now, have Carrie make you some coffee, maybe some breakfast and show you to your desk. I'll be right over."

"Okay. See you soon...Jackson." She hesitates. Gives me the bedroom eyes and bites her lip before exiting.

Shit! Fuck! This is just what I needed. Fine ass woman on the job.

*****

The office is packed up and I now must mentally prepare to give Monica a tour. The hard part about being a boss is restraint. If I impress the board as a member, I can grow and lead my own company within months.

The room is hallow as I reminisce. My very first day as an intern, I had no experience except a degree. I did my best to get to where I am now. I earned every promotion by studying books, the managers, the chairmen and asking questions. Most of my employees didn't like me, but who gives a fuck. Now, I made it to the top. I wonder where those losers are. I smile at my Mac Computer. It harbors all the hard work and dedication I put in this room from HTML's to Coding for the company website.

A tear escapes as I remember all the engagements from congrats from my teammates, when I received full time employment, to meeting people like Tyler. I've come a long way. Then there's sharing the news with Clare. She has always been proud. I have been doing all of this for us. Now look where we stand...

Knock, knock. My thoughts are interrupted.

"Hey, Sorry to intrude Jackson, but now is the time to lock up and help Monica," Carrie says.

"I wipe my face. Sorry, was having a moment to appreciate how far I've come. I'll be right out."

"Sure thing. She's at her desk."

I use the handkerchief in my coat pocket to wipe my face. I turn off the lights and head to Monica. While I walk, I pass co-workers, thanking me for inspiring them and congratulating me on getting chair. I shake many hands as I walk.

I approach Monica's desk and she is adjusting a frame. Her breasts, voluptuous, staring at me. I lick my lips. She looks up. Her skin is glistening. "Oh, Hey Chairman. I see you're finally done. Must we begin?" The corners of her lips peel open as she speaks. She's happy to see me.

I smile. "Sure thing. Let's start with the office that controls all the wiring for this place."

She loops her arm in mine and I hesitate. I don't want to snatch her hand off, then again, I do. I don't need any rumors going around about the new girl and me. When we reach the control room, I release her arm, gently. She's in awe. She also has a notepad, which I must have missed, and she starts jotting down something.

"Whatcha' doin' with that?" I ask.

"Oh, I'm making suggestions based on the organization of this place. I not only want to get hands on in IT but want to improve some functions in this office."

244

Thinking, I just shrug. She can discuss it with me and the team at a board meeting. I continue the tour, showing her the breakroom, the game room; recently added to relieve stress, the supervisor's offices and where assistants are at all times. I also show her the restrooms.

"I believe I covered everything," I say to Monica.

"Aw. Tour over so soon. What about downstairs?"

I'm not sure who told her about any other level of this company, but I say, "well we don't really go downstairs. And upstairs is for the board members."

She smiles. "Thank you, Jackson. This has been fun." She writes on her pad. "I'll be in touch if I have any other questions." She grabs my pointer finger with her hand. A spark sends vibrations through my body.

"If you don't mind, I have to go make a call," I

look directly in her eyes. There's a hint of disappointment as I walk away.

Behind me, she yells "Ok boss. See you later!"

I call Kevin, whom is Tyler's assistant now. Tell him to have Tyler meet me at noon. Which is coming up fast. We need to talk over lunch.

Tyler arrives in my empty office fifteen minutes after I called. I brief him on the week's schedule from meetings to sites for computer adjustments around town. I notify him that a Janice needs a visit at her job to update their systems. His eyebrows are raised so I ask, "Why the curiosity in your eyes?"

He sits on the edge the table. "Nothing. Just the name sounds familiar. I'm on it though."

"Okay. Sounds good. Oh, we have a female tech, her name is Monica. Keep the reputation up by showing her good hospitality."

He smirks. "You got it."

"Yo T. Why are you so short with me today? Everything chill?"

He looks at the room then back at me, " Yeah bro. Just a lot on my mind. My dad died, my mom is staying over, the party the other day..."

I put a hand on his shoulder. "My man. You have to take it easy. One issue at a time. Want to talk over this food?"

Chinese food has been delivered, I ordered sesame chicken, fried rice, honey bbq chicken and lo mein. He says, "Sure. Why not." Then he sits down.

Our lunch was meaningful and interesting. This the first time he's told me about his life without joking. He even mentioned how he thinks this Janice is the one he met at Central Park the other day. A little too coincidental, but that's not my business. Before he takes off, he tips off that he had a phenomenal date with a beautiful lady and is starting to fall for her but

247

refuse to give any added information because he is unsure if she feels the same. I tell him, "Fight for her if she's truly worth it." He gives me a smug look then finishes eating.

After lunch, he leaves, and I call Clare. She picks up on the first ring. I'm talking to her as if no time has been between us, but my heart and mind is guilty. Monica is invading my space. She shouldn't, not when I've had bomb ass sex with Clare the other day. I tell her about the new employees, embellish a little so she doesn't get insecure. I tell her we have male and female new hires. But man, is my stomach in knots.

She's telling me about her workday as I lock up. I walk to the elevator to go upstairs to my new desk. I have to get into some new work. When I get to my desk, the sun is blazing. I have full clearance to outside as the windows reflect my attire. It's a beautiful view...of myself... and this new location. The skyscrapers across the way, bring joy to my heart. I head to my desktop to set up, entering my password. Clare geeks out about exceeding sales and I tell her that's great, but I have to go, and we will talk later.

After hanging up, I inhale. Thank God for my new blessings and get to work. The first thing I pull up is the new software I'm working on. It's a format I am sure most users will appreciate it. It's like Microsoft office and the internet template as a hybrid app, conjoining the functionality of both, for files/documents to be swapped and alternated in tabs, yet automatically saved.

I have been working on this while I was an associate. No one knows about this because I wanted it to be complete. I plan to present it at the next chair meeting. I adjust some coding so users can also play around with the color of their templates. I have to do some work on the company website. I'm in my zone when I get a call. I click line 1 on the intercom, "Talk to me."

"Hey Jackson. It's me. I was hoping I can come in the office and talk to you about something?"

"Sure come in 10 minutes if it can wait. I'm working on a project."

Silence. Then she says, "Alright boss. See you soon." I just know she smiled.

Monica.

I hesitate as I stare at the phone after the call ends. I pull up the prospectus for renovating the website. I walk over to my box that is labeled "Urgent." It has the mood board I drafted for the website. I review it over, then insert most of it onto the computer to send to the visual designers. Then I draft up the sitemaps, and user interface. I prepare the bugs and firewall for the site. I stop working, saving all my work as the knock finally occurred at my door.

She's here.

"Do you have a minute? I wanted to get some suggestions from you. What are you working on?"

"Well, hello Monica," she smiles. I say, "A website. I don't want to share the details just yet. But I can show you how to set up a software for yourself."

She walks over, and her heels are clacking as she gets closer. She sits on the desk. I try not to let the temptation get to me and direct my focus to the screen. I pull up an old software to show her some of the work I've done. Her hand brushes across my hand on the mouse.

She turns her attention to me. "Oouu, you're soooo good at this. It's sexy." She slides off the desk, onto my lap, straddles me. Then she plays with my tie. "What else do you have to give?"

Her hands glide down my shirt. She's getting lower. I should stop her, but she's so fine. My dick is pulsating as she unzips my pants. "Monica...what are you doing?"

"Oh, I didn't come here to learn tech sweetie. I came here to give you what I know you want. I saw the way you looked at me earlier."

That's the last thing she said before her warm lips wrap around my dick. She's bobbin' up and down, saliva gushes sound louder than it is. The heat of getting caught, is making me enjoy this even more. She's moaning and turning me on more. I am fighting the urge to grunt, kinda hard though since she is going faster and deeper with each stroke. She whips her tongue on my shaft. She's sucking like I'm a sour apple blow pop lollipop.

A soft moan escapes my lips. "Damn, Monica. Fuucckkk."

She ignores me and goes faster. I cum quickly. Just in time because I got a phone call and a knock on the door. Monica gets up, cleans her mouth, and sits back on the desk. I zip up and fix my face.

She gets the door, mentioning "data visualization" as a decoy conversation. She smirks. Monica waves goodbye, I wave back.

I nod my head and get the phone. "Jackson speaking." Tyler asks if I can meet him downstairs. I tell him I'll come shortly, I put one finger up as I'm on the phone. Carrie comes in and sits on a chair.

What do she want?

Chapter Twenty-Five

CLARE

Ever since Nicole seen Tyler, she's been asking me about him. She thinks he is so fine and is desperately trying to pry to get his number. I tell her he is seeing someone.

Not me claiming ol' dude already! Haha, in a way I have the right as he just finger fucked me before work. A smile trickles on my face. I am flustered just reminiscing and it happened just 10 minutes ago. I walk away from Nicole, cheery and think about what just happened. Girls should fawn over Ty, he's very handsome. I spray *Love Spell* by *Victoria's Secret* before starting my shift. I put my things in the locker, then go to my station. Nicole and Stacy are next to me at the cashier area, still gawking over Tyler and trying to manifest his arrival.

I tremble and accidentally knock over the scanner. They laugh and I make a joke, "My bad girls. I'm feeling clumsy right now. I might need coffee!" We all laugh in unison.

The day is busy and steady. Not much room for a 5-minute break. Sales are booming as people are collecting books from the "New Release," and "Bestseller" tables. At this rate, the store will beat usual daily sales.

*****

Store goal overachieved! I sold 75 memberships. I persuade the customers that if they're going to frequent B&N, then they should reap the benefits which has discounts and heads up on new releases. I tell them I own one myself because I love to read. I love seeing customers happy. Even in the cafe, their goal has been fantastic, with the cookies selling the most besides coffee. I grab me an Iced Grande White Mocha, a little delightful change, and a sugar cookie. On my way to the breakroom, I text Jackson.

Still thinking about that night. Sex was amazing,

you're still amazing, but the sex was just release for both of us. I don't know if I'm ready to forget what happened even though it was my fault. Love you.

When I get downstairs, there's a package for me. It's roses and Edible arrangements. I smile. It says, "See you after work." That damn Tyler!

Nicole nosy ass comes over, "Oooo who's that from?"

I crinkle up the paper. I say, "Oh. Um. Jackson, he misses me." Damn she's nosy as hell!

"Alright now! Girl you so lucky!" She walks away.

Thank Goodness! I put it away and continue my shift. After work, I check my messages. Jackson said,

Baby, that was amazing. You finished me. I'll give you your time. However, we need to talk. Call me when you can.

I laugh and head to Nick's shop. He starts

smiling the minute the bell chimes. He is giving me the gossip look, leaning on the counter with his face in his hands. I approach him with a fair greeting, a hug, and our new handshake.

Nick says, "Bittccchhhh! Don't hate me ok, I just work here. But Tyler came in and Gurl, he is foine. Like super fine. I see why he around. I think he's my new fantasy man, you can keep Jackson. Is Tyler...bi-sexual?"

I start crackin' up. I slam my hand on the table, in joy. "Omg Nick! First off, N-O! He only likes punani! And second, good! Get ya eyes and ya cock off my Jackson. Finally!!"

He chuckles. He playfully slaps my arm. "Girl stop. I know you like Tyler. You got fans. But excuse me while I take the next customer."

I blush and step aside. When the customer leaves, I ask. "Should I meet him tonight?"

Nick says, "Oh no honey. I'm not getting involved in your business. Jackson stops in here too. You know I hate lying to that caramel blessed skin." He pouts.

I laugh. "Fine. I'm going. I'll tell you all the deetz later boo. I'm gone."

He hands me an energy bar. He says, "Here take this. It's something new I'm working on to build more customers. Tell me what you think and how much energy it gives you."

It's double chocolate chip. I thank him and walk out. I work my remaining shift and take my *Edible arrangements* roses as I clock out. Nicole leaves after me so luckily, she won't be in my business.

Of course, as if he just knew, Tyler is waiting. His knee bent, chillin', on his passenger door, and looking sexy ass ever.

I hadn't realized Nick was behind me as I froze seeing Tyler. Nick says, "Go on Girl. That's a real man, waiting for you and shit. Hmph. Where is Jackson like this?"

We laugh. I walk toward Tyler, hoping I don't fall.

He smiles upon my arrival. "Welcome to the bat mobile," he jokes.

"Shut up," I laugh and get in. I place the items on the backseat, I ate most of the fruits during small breaks on the job.

Tyler walks over to the driver's side. When he's strapped in and ready to go, he looks at me.

"Do you mind if we go to 1,2,3 Burger?"

"As you wish, boo boo," he says. "So, how was your day?"

"Oh. It was great! Thank you for the gift," I say.

He touches my shoulder, "Not a problem." He plays some music. *Pandora* is on shuffle. "Anywhere, by 112" is playing. He starts singing and I wonder if it's a hint. I try not to dwell on it as the GPS says five minutes. However, my mind trails to when I fantasized about us when I took the *Uber* with a different driver.

We find parking and enter the sports bar. There are 2 seats at the bar, so we sit down. Tyler wastes no time. He orders 5 for $5 shots. Then he looks at me, ready to share what's been on his mind since this morning.

He cuts right into it. "My dad died--"

"I'm so sorry Tyler, that's awful! Now I see why you wanted to talk."

"It's all good. My mom is at my house for some time."

"Aw I can understand her grief--are you two...close?" I say as I'm waving the bartender down.

"He says, "Yeah, I love my mom to pieces. But I don't want her staying too long. I like my space. She can stay maybe another week then we are going to figure out what to do now that dad's gone."

"I'm sorry but Tyler I have to laugh," I chuckle. "No, you are not throwing mom dukes out after she lost her husband! You are trippin'."

He grabs my left hand. "Boo, I know. But we know I'm a little fucked up." He snickers.

"Besides, how am I supposed to get some punani if she in my crib?"

I blush. "Uh-yeah. I hear you. Just be kind to her, okay?" I smile. I squeeze his right leg.

Tyler jerks. Adjusts his shirt. He is uncomfortable after my leg squeeze. The bartender comes, and I order an Amaretto sour. Tyler asks for whiskey on the rocks.

"So, Tyler, what was this morning about?" I bite my lip.

"I wanted to give you the best day with a sunrise surprise, that's all."

"Well, it was on my mind all day at work. I think you succeeded," I take a sip. "Work was amazing. Not to change the subject, but it was! Sales boomed around the store. A very rare accomplishment. I had lots of energy, was super charged, and selling memberships like crazy---"

Tyler kisses me. In shock, excited, and horny, I kiss back. His tongue slips to mine and in unison our tongues are passionate. I stop him before I take him down at this bar stool. "Tyler I'm going to the bathroom, be right back."

His eyes are low, he stares at me and says "Okay."

I walk to the bathroom, the door closes behind me. I look in the mirror. The alcohol is getting to me. I smile at my reflection. The door opens and it's Tyler.

He locks the door behind him. Before I get a word out, he rushes to me, and we make out. I should stop, this is so wrong. But it feels so good.

He sticks his fingers under my dress and inside my panties. He whispers, "Take these off," then he moans.

I do as he say and then he unzips his pants, pull them down and off. He kisses me again, hikes my leg on the sink counter and I feel his dick ease inside. I'm already wet from all the kissing and finger teasing. I moan, slightly loud. He puts two fingers on my mouth to shush me. I put them in my mouth, and he grinds harder. He lifts my other leg, wraps both around his waist and holds me as he continues to fuck me. When I cum, he releases me then his head makes his way down to feast. He looks up and says, "I'm not done with you yet."

I wonder why no one has come to use the bathroom yet but the thought is short lived as the slivers of his tongue feel so amazing. I move my hips to the rhythm of his oral movements. "Ty...oh God!!!" A strong release flushes down and he scoops it all in his mouth. I use my two hands to lift him up. It's my turn. I flip him to lean near the wall then I go down on him.

Tyler groans, immediately. "Fuuccckkkk Clare!!!" His hands are on my head, "Damn, this feels good," he hisses.

I have one hand stroking his shaft, while I'm bobbing up and down. I do a tongue twister and his body pulsates with my mouth. He lifts me up and turns me over, I bend and perk my ass.

He says, "That's how you do me baby? Ok watch thissss...." he slips in between my thighs. He is fucking me gooood. The rhythmic pattern is hot, sexy, arousing, breathtaking. I need more.

His pounding gets faster, and I can't hold back anymore. He's groaning. "Clare....shit.... you feel so guh-good..."

"Uh, uh! Ooouuuu! You...tooooo! I'm cumin'" I blurt out.

We moan in unison and cum together. He

kisses me once more then he gets dressed. I wash my hands and my face then use the bathroom.

He says, "I'll meet you at the bar, before anyone gets more suspicious."

I yell, "Okay! See you soon!" Afterwards, I pee and wipe. I rewash my hands and walk out. I realize I didn't put my panties back on, but I think they have been tainted by the bathroom floor already. So, I'm not going back for them. Then again, I didn't see them near the sink...maybe Tyler picked them up, who cares. It'll give him something to remember me by. I feel like I'm doing the walk of shame back to our seats, although no one is looking at me. Everyone is shouting at the football game that's on the TV and talking among their company.

Tyler smirks as I sit down. He says, "Another drink, Clare bear?"

"Why not?" I say.

Oh boy! What have I done?

Chapter Twenty-Six

TYLER

When my mom told me about the affair, I was almost hurt. But I know women cheat as revenge, so she did it because my dad cheated first and with my best friend's mother. Her pain after we talked about my dad, was hard to watch. I don't like to see her cry. I held her to comfort her, and when she felt better, we watched *Family Feud*. I was grateful to see her smile before I got ready to get ready for Clare. I told my mom to call me if she needed me, but I truly hoped she wouldn't.

On my way to meet Clare at work, I think about how we are going to engage at the bar. I park right by Nick's shop and wait for her. When she came out the store, I smiled. Clare is so stunning. She greets me and as usual she gets in my car. I happily get in the driver's side, and she requests *1,2,3 Burger*. Once we arrive, we make our way to the bar for drinks. As I share the passing of my dad, I can see the concern on her face. I know why Jackson is so in love with her. She has true compassion and sympathy for others. I try to mask my pain by drinking more and talking about her workday. Clare having a good day means everything is okay.

So, when she goes to the restroom, I feel frisky. There's something in this liquor, as the tightening of my chest has me wanting to inhale the air Clare breathes. I want to be consumed by her body. Since everyone is minding their business, I casually walk to the restroom.

I look back and open the door. I lock it behind me as she stares at herself in the mirror. The tension in the room allows me to make out with her. She's submitting to my actions as I continue to play with her body. My hand slips under her dress and into her panties while she takes a deep breath. She's so freakin' wet, and it is turning me on. I ease her panties down and keep kissing her. Her invitation speaks volumes as I put her leg up on the counter and fuck her.

Our bodies have been asking for this and I couldn't feel more satisfied. Clare feels effin' good, I don't want to cum yet, even though her moaning is making want to. I stop to give her head, just yearning taste her. Clare's sweetness tastes like sugar. I lick her up and scoop up all her fluids into my mouth with my tongue. Her orgasm increases even more and I'm hungry. After her release, she lifts me up and I want to dive back in.

However, she takes over me. Her mouth wraps around my dick and sets my body on fire. I try not to yell as we are in public but she's fuckin great at sucking dick. After a couple more mouth strokes I lift her up then fuck her from behind. We both nut together then I quickly snatch her panties off the floor as I put my pants back on.

She ran to the toilet, perfect time to head to the bar. I go to our seats and drink a whiskey sour I request the minute I sit down. The bartender looks at me with weary, but smiles. Either he knows what's up or find me cute, just like Nick. Either way I give him a head nod and wait for Clare. After five minutes, she joins me.

She accepts another drink. On her face is a question. We sit in silence for a while. Her drink comes, a Margarita. She sips and I watch her lips grab the straw. I bite my lip in response.

"Do you want to get home after this? I assume you have to work in the morning, as do I."

She looks at me. "Aw, I'm having so much fun. You're right. I do have to work tomorrow. A double at that. Ugh. Fine take me home after this drink." She laughs.

"Of course bug-a-boo. This has been fun," I say. My phone is vibrating in my pocket, but I ignore it.

"You gonna get that? Could be important." Clare asks.

"Nah. They can leave a voicemail. I only have

attention for you."

She shuffles around on her stool. As she is panty less, I'd love to be the bar stool.

I ask her about a childhood memory she uses as a trigger to calm her down, a conversation starter before we leave. She starts talking and I stare. I wonder if Jackson talks to her like this or is it just about work. Clare goes on about sitting in Central Park by herself every day after high school. I think about when she seen me at work with Jackson. She hasn't mentioned it since. I should tell her about my new position. In the car, I will.

****

In the car I check my phone. My mom called; I'll call her back after dropping Clare off. I put music on *Pandora* on shuffle and tell her about my new position replacing Jackson, as he got promoted. Bursts of excitement radiates on her face, the joy in her smile. She tells me Jackson mentioned it earlier after he explained that he had to tour two new employees. Pondering if I should tell her there is only a female, I don't. Jackson's lie can keep up until it blows over in his face. I tell her that it feels good to be trusted to climb the corporate ladder.

She invites me in for a celebratory drink and that's a bad idea. Especially after what happened at the bar, I don't think she's ready for more. I park the car and escort her to the door. The look in her eyes is begging me to come in. I take one step, then my phone rings.

"I'm sorry. I really want to. My mom keeps calling. I should head home and make sure she's alright. I'll text you and if you're still awake...I can swing back over here."

She laughs. "Oh my God, yes! Go make sure your mother is well. You got my number...taxi driver." She winks as she enters her building.

I head back to the car and text my mother that I'm on my way. I look back at the empty space,

Clare was just at and smile. I'll be back to you my dear! My inner thoughts becoming frisky. I fly home. I hope nothing bad has happened.

Chapter Twenty-Seven

JACKSON

I'm lying-in bed thinking about the workday. I don't know if it was my cologne, my suit, or the new job title, but the ladies have been all over me. Monica has been a nice surprise. Shockingly so, I want to put her on top of me and have her ride it like a rodeo. The office oral sex was sexy. Carrie had come in to ruin our time, just to make moves on me as well. She grabbed my hand, told me to get up off my seat and took me to my mood board

I had set on the table near the window. She had made chit chat about whatever I'm working on is so hot, like the view in my office. I let go of her hand to close my project, as it isn't ready yet. She knocked over the pen case, on purpose...almost as if she wanted me to pull her panties down to fuck her. Carrie is cute, but I'm not feeling her. I walked back to my desk to sit down, and she gave me a kiss on my cheek, telling me congratulations on my new promotion.

I looked at her until she walked out, then took a breath. I continued my day, working on the website. Once 5pm hit, I was gone. I flew home just to undress, drink and relax. Then I took a meaningful shower. I told Clare the news and I knew I shouldn't have told a half truth, but I didn't need her coming to the office the next day. I might do a half day tomorrow, work a little at home.

I sip this bourbon and think about Monica. The oral transaction in my office was so hot, it was the thrill of getting caught. I feel almost like a slut. I laugh to myself. I just fucked Clare, then got head from Monica the new girl. Now work is going to be intriguing. The new promotion has me as a ladies' man. I text the boys in our group chat as I light a blunt.

Me: Yo we need to talk! Let's link up soon. There's a bubble showing a response coming.

Q: Aw shit. Jack calling a meeting. What one of y'all niggas done did? Lol

Mark: Shut up Q. Maybe it's yo ass. Anyways I'm game. Say where and when. Let's allow Sal to choose this time.

Sal: Wassup negros. Aight, I'll holla at y'all in a few. I'm a little occupied with this new tail I just met.

Me: Sal, you got til tomorrow bruh before you're not in charge no more.

Everyone laughs in the chat. I puff, inhale, and take another hit of this weed. Shit strong as hell. Coupled with the bourbon, my night is going well, just missing some pussy. I should call Clare.

Clare's phone is going to voicemail. Why isn't she picking' up the phone? I don't dwell too much on it, instead I turn the TV on. *Good Times* is on. I leave it on to kill time. I hope Sal choose a spot with good whiskey.

Two hours pass by, and I get off the couch, go take a leak wash my hands then get fresh to be on my way to see Clare. I put on white tee and grey sweatpants with my fresh white ups. I brush my waves. Heading to the door, I grab my keys, phone, and a bottle of water. I shoot her a text,

I'm on my way babe. Miss you.

I rev up the car and take off. I get to Clare's house in 15 minutes with no traffic. I park and check my phone. No messages. I look up to see a car, like Tyler's near her house. I squint my eyes but can't see who's inside the car. I lurk and see if she comes out to get in the car. After 10 minutes, she comes out, lock up and looks both ways before heading to the right, to walk down the block. I quickly leave my car to confront her. The other car that was lingering, took off in a haste. I made a mental note to run Tyler's location at work tomorrow. Besides what would he be doing here? Anyways, I abruptly stop Clare. She's surprised to see me.

"Where you going?" I say, leaning in to kiss her.

She jumps. Then she kisses me back and gives me a hug. Everything feels...forced. "Jackson! What a... surprise. I'm on my way to Kayla's, sorry if I haven't gotten back to you yet I was in a hurry to get changed for girl's night."

I look at her fit. She's wearing a white tube top, black leather leggings and black wedges with her leather jacket. She looks good. I want to convince her we should have a quickie, but I know she's going to say no.

"Oh. I did worry about you. That's why I flew over here to see you," I say, holding her hand.

She picks up her other hand and cups my face. "Jackson baby, you're so kind. I promise you I'm great. Having a wonderful day. We can meet up tomorrow and I'll give you a key copy. Promise. Now I have to go."

I look into her beautiful eyes. She still loves

me. I try not to cry. I feel guilty for my secret endeavors with Monica. Clare is a good woman. I look at Clare, "I'll let you go. I'll be back tomorrow. Bright and early!" I turn to leave, stalling before saying, "I love you, Clare."

She says, "I love you, Jackson." She smiles and walks away.

I walk back to my car. I sit there for a few minutes and decide to follow her, just to make sure she is getting to the subway safely. However, what I see is what I didn't expect.

Chapter Twenty-Eight

CLARE

I can't believe how rowdy I've been in just a week. Is this hoe phase part 2? I thought we only get one of those. I knew I wanted to have sex with Tyler the day I got in his cab. Did I mean for it to happen at a bar? Absolutely not. But man was it sexy. I needed more. It was unlike anything I've had before. After sex, I ran to the stall and fanned myself. I was burning up! Don't get me wrong, Jackson is a great lover, but there is something about wanting what you shouldn't have.

My pussy invited him inside my home, good thing he said no. Because paranoia would hit fast, Jackson can show up at any time. When Tyler said to let him go home first, I silently "phewed" so I can get in, shower, and lay down. I watched him get in his car then went in. I took off all my clothes and went to the shower. I don't remember locking the door. Thirty minutes flew by when my mind told me to just go with it. Wrapping myself in my towel, I head to my phone to text Tyler,

Meet me at Days Inn.

To my surprise, he writes back instantly.

My mother only needed me for a short amount of time. I'm actually outside, down the block...I have a new model car for the night, lent my mom the cab car. Lol. Same color, new plates. I'll blink so you'll notice. Didn't want your bug-a-boo to see me.

Relief and joy succumb me. I dry off and get dressed. I'm feeling leather today; white tube top, black leather leggings and black wedges with her leather jacket. I look and feel bad ass! I grab all my essentials, head out and walk toward his direction. I'm stopped and the touch, makes the presence familiar. Jackson...

I have to think on the fly so the first thing I say is I'm going to Kayla's house. Shit! Now I have to text her to keep up with my alibi!! I shoot her a text before I forget.

Hey baby cakes. I need you to do me a favor. Please, please puh-lease!!! If Jackson ever decides to ask you about tonight, I was at your house. Mhmkay? I'll explain later. Love you!

Jackson insinuates he will return tomorrow, and I offer up giving him the key I promised a while ago. I'm rushing this convo so I can press on. He feels it, I think. *Shouldn't I be nicer?* This is my man! Damn it. I inhale. Quick self-check in and then give him some affection. We quick kissed and hugged before leaving.

My "I love you," is genuine and a lead off to exit. I cannot look at Jackson, without the slight guilt of the bathroom sex with Tyler this afternoon. Hopefully all my lies don't kick me in my ass.

When Jackson walks away to his car, I walk toward Tyler and find the car. I get in and tell him to put on the black baseball hat I had in my purse. For safety measures. I just told him Jackson held me up. He showed up and I couldn't just brush him off so fast.

Tyler looks at me, "You know I have all the time in the world for you. You're here with me now. Enough about your reality, I'm fantasy baby." He licks his lips. My legs clench together.

He takes off. "To Days Inn, Brooklyn we go."

I smirk. "Yes. To continue where you left off."

He laughs.

I turn on the radio. Chris Brown's "Loyal," is on. I chuckle. Perfect timing.

Tyler and I look at each other and start singing along.

****

As he pulls into the parking lot, I'm nervous. My legs are shaking, my breathing picks up and my palms are sweaty. Tyler looks at me as he turns the car off.

"You, ok?"

"Uh yeah. Just anxious," I say while squeezing my hands together.

"I can tell. Your whole body is in a mood. Having change of heart?"

"No. No. It's just been a while since I've done any of this since..." I pause.

"Right. Got it. Shall we?" He says, exciting the car to open my door.

I breathe. Five quick breaths. I grab his hand and we walk to the entrance. He presses the button to lock the door. Inside, the bellman greets us. Tyler speaks. "Room for 2 please."

I nod, looking around. The man enters information on his desktop, Tyler pays for the room, and we are granted keys to room 105. Tyler has his arm around me. He hands me he key. "Ready sweetness? Go 'head."

I say, "Yes. I can't believe we're here. We're doing this!" I open the door. The color scheme is cute, a peachy yellow paint on the walls, with matching sheets and cover on the bed. There's a TV on the wall and a king size bed across from it. There's a mini fridge under a desk underneath the TV. A nightstand with the Bible inside resides next to the bed. God will probably punish us as we sin. I take a look at the bathroom, and everything looks clean. I turn around and Tyler is undressing. A small snicker leaves my mouth.

He says, "Just getting comfy," he pats the bed. "Join me."

I undress, slowly. I reveal a yellow bra and panties set. "Rawr," I joke.

Tyler's glaring at me. "OW! OW! Get over here gurl!"

I cat crawl over to Tyler. He's biting his lips. I straddle him, rock back and forth. I take off his T-shirt. Then I kiss him, nibbling on his bottom lip. His dick is getting hard as I divide our mouths with my tongue. He groans. I dry hump him a little longer then kiss my way down to his boxers.

I'm ready! I think to myself, in my Trey Songz voice.

Chapter Twenty-Nine

TYLER

My mother wanted to make sure I was okay. That's what she does, always puts everyone else first. I asked her if she was doing okay and when she said yes, I handed her the keys to my car. I already went and purchased a Mercedes Benz, just picked it up. It was time for my mom to enjoy herself again.

When Clare texted me about Jackson, I frowned. But no matter as I remained cool. I reached Clare's house in no time after my mother almost suffocated me with the happiest of hugs. Mom probably thinks I have commitment issues since I'm always leaving, but we can blame my dad. As I get to Clare's house, I see a car nearby, assuming it is Jackson, I keep on driving.

Having Clare in my car, made me want to tear her up before the hotel. She gave me a hat to disguise myself and I thought about those murder shows on TV. As I was driving, I thought he was following us, so I made a few turns off the navigation. Clare was too busy jammin' with her eyes closed to notice.

We get to the hotel, and I park up. My dick is charged and ready to go. But I had to put my IT charm on and get us in the room. The ambiance was very nice. I hadn't expected it to be so clean. But it's rated better than the other hotels in the town.

Clare takes her clothes off so anxiously. Her leather ensemble is divine, I might just have to add the panties to my collection. I stare at her as she makes a nerd joke and sexily comes to me. When I told her to come to me, it was as if I channeled a new woman. The look in her eyes says passion, I stare back as I'm feeling the same. She climbs on top of me, and my member is rising to the occasion. She leads as she makes out with me then trails her head down to my shaft.

I look at her so impressed and excited. Deep

into the zone, I hadn't realized she stopped after some couple of minutes or maybe almost an hour, shit I'm a little turnt...until I felt the warmth of her pussy hug my dick. My mind trails to "Pony" by Genuine when she climbs on top of me. I grip her waist and slow whine underneath her. The air is too hot, I think I'm catching feelings. After she rides me like a rodeo, I kiss her. I need control, doggy style is that position. I lick her supple nipples, turning them hard. I whisper, "turn around," and jerk my hard on.

She hops off me and I insert her. The sounds of me clappin' cheeks, turns me on more. I go faster, harder, yet careful so I don't cum fast. She's panting and moaning. I groan and tell her let them screams loose. Tons of "Oh baby," and "Yes daddy T," exploits from her mouth. She is moaning louder, and I feel like Trey Songz, because the neighbors definitely know my name.

45 minutes later, she's sleep, and I am watching a repeat basketball game that is almost

done. I brush the hair on the side of her face and kiss her cheek. I get up to drink some water. Once the game ends, I hop in the shower.

I bask in the heat. I wash up and dry off after fifteen minutes. She's still out like a light. I'm shocked she hasn't asked about her panties from the bar. I walk over to the lingerie that's laid on the floor and intake her scent. Fruity mixed with her sweet nectar. I won't collect these, I'll let the memory sink in my mind. I throw on boxers and a fresh Tee, then cuddle her in bed. I'm getting hard just looking at her. Maybe she won't mind if I start up another round.....I chuckle.

****

I must of fell asleep to my thoughts because I'm awake and blinded by the sun.... but not only that... I'm getting morning pleasure. I look down and Clare is giving me head. I look to my left and the clock says 7 A.M. and on the right by the door is breakfast, yet I didn't hear room service. Here I am in a room, getting reserviced. "Shiiiiiiii-" I moan. She's too good at this shit man. Such a nice wake up alarm. I cum once she does her tongue twister and say, "Well good morning to you too."

She wipes her face and swallows. A gasp escapes my lips. She says, "Good morning. I enjoyed last night and wanted to Thank you. Ready to eat?"

"Which part?" My mind says out loud, without permission.

"Breakfast silly," Clare says while laughing. She hands me cheesy eggs, apple cinnamon waffles and maple bacon on a plate with French vanilla coffee. She kisses me on my cheek.

I say, "Thank you," and bite into the bacon. She sits next to me and eats her food too.

Silence consumes us as we eat and drink coffee. No need for words when we have been hungry all night. After breakfast she cleans up, "Well I should shower so I can get home and get changed for work." Still naked, she sashays to the shower.

I nibble on my bottom lip. "One's for the money, two's for the show, three's to get busy and four's out the door..." I sing in my head as I enter the shower behind her.

****

Fuckin' in the shower. Such a satisfying thing to do, especially before work. Afterwards, we wash up, I wash her back and she play washes my dick. I dry her off and she dries me off. After brushing our teeth, we get dressed then head to check out. The bellman smiles. I put my arm around her, and we walk to the car.

In the car she tells me about Nick. I told her he wants to be my boyfriend, and we laugh in unison. The ride to her house feels suddenly shorter than when we left last night. Maybe because we talked the whole way here. I double park and she get out.

She leans down, I roll the window down. She says, "Tyler this has been amazing. Enjoy your day at work!" There's a pause as if she wants to say, "With Jackson," but knows that will kill the mood.

I say, "I always have a wonderful time with you dear. Text me! Gotta run!" I wink. She steps back, and I drive off. Working with Jackson is going to be very enlightening.

Chapter Thirty

JACKSON

Instead of walking down the subway steps, Clare hopped in a car instead. She sat in the front, not the back. I questioned it and started to follow them, then I lost them. It's unlike me anyway. I head home and strip naked. I wanted this life with Clare, living together, walking around bare and random sex, laughter, and happiness...in a new apartment of course. I lock the door, then lay on my bed and the sheets feel like clouds. I'm more exhausted than I thought.

I miss Clare. I really cannot wait until the morning. Get work over with, head to Clare on my break. We are working toward forgiveness, a very emotional journey as I know I haven't been the best to her dealing with work, so I can be the best provider I can be. I am doing better, now that I'm promoted, I strive to text her more, see her more and call her. Let me close my eyes so I can be on to the next....

I wake up at 5 A.M. shower and get ready. It's Friday! I'm feeling good. I make a sausage, egg, and cheese on a croissant after getting dressed. I drink some orange juice. I put the dishes in the sink and I'm out by 6 A.M. In the car, the Bluetooth goes off. I press the button to take the call and it's my baby sister Nicole.

"Hey sis. What's going on? Callin' me this early. You good?"

"Big bro! Yeah, I'm good, chillin'. I had to catch you before work, mom told me you be busy. What happened to keepin' up with us? What's goin' on between you and Clare?"

"Sis, not this early. Damn! We will talk about that later. You right, it's been a min since I caught up with y'all. That's my bad. Here, how about when I stop at a red light, I'll set up a group chat for us, including Crystal and Victoria. We can all find the best time to link I'm person. I miss my sisters, especially you baby girl!"

She laughs on the phone. Probably blushing too. Nikki and I have always been the closest. Mom said when she was born, I held her, and we had an automatic bond. I will go hard for any of them though. Victoria and Crystal may be older than us, but I'm a big little bro to them too.

We say, "I love you," as we end the call. I slap the steering wheel. Seeing my family is a must. When I get to work, I have to check my calendar and prioritize my sisters. After the red light, I speed away, getting to work in no time.

*****

On the way up, I'm in the elevator with Tyler and Monica. Silence is illuminating, and Monica winks at me. I smile in return. I say, "Good morning team," glancing at them both.

Tyler gives a head nod. "Morning buddy."

"Morning...uh...sir..." Monica studders.

Tyler gets off on his floor and Monica

breathes. She turns to me. Even steps a few inches closer to me.

I tell her, "Don't. Cameras are watching,"

She stays where she is. She asks, "How are you feeling?"

I keep my eyes straight to avoid her. Out the corner of my eye, I peep her little black dress and yellow heels. Her hair is curly. I bite my lip. "I'm great so far. My sisters called me, begging to see me. So, I have to make that happen. I also need some coffee."

"Well, let me know if I can help! I'll be sure to have Carrie, or someone send you that coffee."

It's our stop and I let her get off before me. She either knows I'm watching or is naturally a seductive walker. Her ass shakes to the rhythm of her heels, and it makes me want an office visit instantly. I make my way to my office and place my suitcase down. I stare out the window. Then I swivel in my chair and turn my computers on.

I'm about to work on the website when I get a knock at my door. Monica brought me a latte. She says, "It's Caramel Macchiato, extra caramel," as she places it down.

I grab her hand. I pull her in my lap and whisper, "this kind of behavior will lead to some very bad things. Thank you for your curiosity. Meet me at 12pm for the meeting about this website." I release her.

She smooths her dress. "Yes sir. Pleasure was all mine. I'll be looking forward to that meeting."

I put a pen in my mouth and watch her leave. I tap it on the desk and open my planner. Let me see if I can make time for family this weekend. I'm thinking Sunday. I make a note.

My phone vibrates. I look and it's Sal. I remind myself to respond after work. He better be gettin' back to me about a place to chill. I have to code this website and reveal creating a blog which will be owned by Monica and whoever else she wants to partner with on it. This can increase our brand, allowing us more time on social media to boost clientele. I am interfacing this site and fixing the HTML, I want the colors to be red, white, and black. Classy, crisp, and professional.

This Caramel Mach is bomb as hell! Monica must have told them to add some love! It's fueling my work. I never felt so alive. But I'm immediately reminded of Clare. *Starbucks* will forever be our spot. I wonder if she ordered a latte. I shake the thought and keep working.

Time is moving too fast as the meeting is quickly approaching. I walk to the room to make sure it's set up with five chairs on each side and a head chair. I walk to the breakroom to grab the muffin basket, and shout for hands on the coffee carafe, water jug refill, cups, plates, and napkins. Three male employees assist. After setting up, I have about 20 minutes before chairwoman Joan shows up. She's always early. I set up the laptop to lead the meeting with my proposals.

My cup in one hand, I pull my phone out to respond to Sal.

My fault, Sal. Caught up at work. Big day. We chillin at yo' crib tonight? Say the word, I'm down. No strippers either! Just boys! Lol

I close our group chat and text my sisters.

Lovely ladies! Let me know if Sunday works for everyone, I miss you gals! I'll come to whoever, wherever. I'm relinquishing control! Haha. Love y'all.

I'm about to text Clare when Monica comes in. I brief her on the blog, so she isn't surprised during the meeting. The humbleness on her face doesn't go unnoticed. Her cheeks turn rosy as a bright smile shows on her face. She's about to thank me. As Tyler interrupts.

He says, "Just wishing you good luck. This is huge bro."

"Thanks man, appreciate you. Take some notes for me, will you?"

"I gotchu'. I know the adrenaline is going to be running."

I give him a dap and turn to the door. The employees and chairmen are filling in, taking seats, and grabbing muffins and coffee. I say, "Hello, Welcome." Watch me ace this meeting.

******

After a 1 hour and 20 minutes, the meeting is done. Everyone is pleased with my ideas and designs. I have a private follow up on Monday. Once everyone leaves, I inhale and exhale. Then I check my phone and prepare to head to lunch. First thing I do outside the office doors is text Clare.

We need to talk about last night. I saw you get in the front seat of a car. Please tell me you are okay? Whose car was that?! Call me - I love you.

I walk to the elevator. I think I'll have *Wendy*'s for lunch. I slide my headphones in and put my *Pandora* radio on shuffle. It's a private ride down.

I'm a little disappointed, was hoping for female company. I walk toward *Wendy's*. It's ten minutes from here, I pass the *Nike* store, *Taco Bell*, and *Journey's*. When I walk inside, my phone goes off. I answer without checking the name.

Monica's on the line. She tells me great work on the presentation and is thrilled I put her in charge of the blog over Carrie. She said she will wait for my return to my office...that can only mean one thing.

I laugh. Unconsciously scratch my head as I say, "I will be back shortly. Shall I get you anything while I'm out?"

She says excitedly, "Oouu bring me a frosty please!"

"You got it." I end the call.

What the fuck am I doing!?

Chapter Thirty-One

CLARE

I watch Tyler drive off then walk inside. I turn my phone off for a while. No way in hell I'm going in today. I walk to the wine cabinet, grab a wine glass, and pour me a drink. I sit at my breakfast nook and gather my thoughts on what a night I just had. Even this morning. It wasn't my intention to give him head, but he was lookin' so fine, and his dick had that morning wood. I just couldn't let it go. Then the sex in the shower...ooouuu weeee!! Man, that man can fuck!

I guzzle the rest of what's in the cup and walk over to the couch. I rest my eyelids. My mind shifts between Jackson and Tyler. Shit. I have to text Jackson. I'll get to that later. This couch feels good. It feels like forever since I laid here. I am tired, but I open this book, *Cheaper to Keep Her* by Kiki Swanson. I get 20 pages in, then my eyelids begin to feel heavy.

Initially, I don't sit still long enough to enjoy my house most times. I turn my phone on. It loads back to its existence. I rest it on my chest. I take my pants off and unfasten my bra. I return to restoring my eyes, I'm getting sleepy...

I definitely fell asleep because my phone is going off. I just missed 10 calls from Kayla. There's also a text that says,

Bitch! Where are you? Did he kidnap you? Are you dick whipped?! And you didn't work today?!! Intentional huh? I thought you was scheduled today. We need to talk! Stop ignoring my calls and call me. Love you chica!

I rub my eyes. I head to the fridge and take out a bottle of water and take a sip. A quick breath then I go to the call log and call Tyler. He doesn't answer so I call Kayla back. She answers immediately.

"Clare! You little whore! About damn time-"

I interrupt. "Ugh shut up already. I had a glass

of wine and laid down, so into my own thoughts. I even turned my phone off to escape from your annoying ass a bit."

She laughs. "Damn the dick must have been too damn good. Since you're home, can I come by?"

"Do I have much of a choice?" I say, sipping water.

"Girl, you already know I don't take no for an answer. See you in 5." Kayla ends the call.

I look at my phone. Kayla is a hot mess. She couldn't warn me first! What if I was being a hoe and had Jackson over! Which reminds me, let me write him. I text him as I walk to the bedroom to put on pajama pants.

Hey Jackson, I'm great. It was just a ride. You know plenty of uber passengers sit in the front right? Don't trip, it was nothing. He had a pool so I sat in front. I'm fine. Kayla and I had so much fun. How are you? How is work?

The buzzer goes off. I let Kayla inside. She says, "You should give me a key."

I say, "Not a chance. Why everyone wanna key! Bad enough I owe Jackson his spare key."

"Damn. Sis lockin' out her own man," Kayla jokes. We embrace in a hug as I close the door behind her. She sits down on the couch.

I pour two wine glasses. I can't even get into what she's been up to because as I hand her the glass, she shouts, "Spill it!"

Sigh. Time to dig my own grave. I take one long sip. "Hold on I need weed. I go diggin' around my drawers. I always keep a stash around for Jackson. Searching my kitchen, I found it by the silverware. I pat it and say, "Ah ha!" Walking back to Kayla, I say "Ok you roll, and I'll fill you in. Then before the good, good part I need a HUGE puff."

Kayla grabs the weed and the wrapper, and I start from the beginning. It takes 10 minutes and

I'm about to share the details from the hotel sex. I tell her, "Ok pass that dutch. I need it now. Whew chile, I went too far." She hands it to me.

Kayla laughs and drinks her wine. "Girl! Tyler has some hold on you!! Y'all fuckin' like rabbits!"

I smack her arm. "Hush! I don't know how we got here, but we did. And it's been damn good. But I have to stop. I think he's starting to fall for me."

"And how would you know for sure? It could just be the pussy-" Kayla says, gesturing for the blunt.

"True. But he had this look in his eyes last night. It was unlike any other eye contact we've had. Not at the time we fucked at the bar, the car, when he picks me up. It felt...special. But if he loves me then I'm in big ass trouble. I only wanted to have sex, to feel, to feel —"

"Appreciated. Respected. Like someone, well a man is there for you when you need him,"

306

Kayla finishes my thought. "I know girl because I've been there. You know this. Jackson been working so much, you feel misplaced. But I thought you two were working it back out?" She asks.

"We are, kind of. I been pushing him away so I can sort out my feelings for Tyler. I know it's stupid. But I promise I will fix this." I lower my head. Guilt is starting to overwhelm me.

Kayla scoots over to hug me. We sit in silence for a minute. A tear falls down my face. "What am I going to do?" I sniffle, wiping my eyes.

She looks at me. "If you want this to stay between us, I won't tell Calli and Sabrina. We don't even have to meet with them. But I need you to end it with Tyler and work on it with Jackson. Please. He's a good man, just trying to do what any man does. It's rough living in NYC, you know you gotta stay ahead of the cost of living before it get you! Find it in your heart to let it all go. Remember he wanted to marry you; it was you that sabotaged it."

"Damn Kay. You read me," I roll my eyes, jokingly. "You're right. I'll make things right in my life. I promise. Thanks bitch," I laugh. "Cheating was a mistake. How do you think Ty will take it?" I pout, inhale the weed.

"Oh girl, I don't know. I just hope this one is an easy drop. If not let me know, I'll handle it."

We laugh together. Drink and smoke some more. Then I say, "I have to get Jackson and his boys to link up with us girl. It's time for a super group meeting."

"Yes girl, count me in. That fine ass Q." Kayla bites her lip.

"EW. Don't! I cannot." I get off the couch, crackin' up and go get another bottle.

Kayla turns the TV on and puts on the movie *Love and Basketball*. We sit and watch, laughing and adding our dialogue along the way. Hanging out, just the two of us like we used to do when we didn't want to hang with Cal and Brina.

****

During the movie, my phone goes off. Kayla glances at it and shakes her head. I gesture for her to hand it to me. She grabs it off the coffee table and gives it to me. It's Jackson calling.

Kayla whispers, "Answer it."

I sigh. "Hello? Hey Jack, babe. How are you?"

His voice sounds like he is smiling. "Clare baby. Thought you'd blow me off again. I'm good and you?"

"I'm good. Hanging with Kayla. You know the vibes," I laugh. I hear him laugh on the other end.

Kayla gives me a thumbs up, then notions to speed it up. I shush her. Tuning back in, he asked me a question and I missed it. "Can you repeat that? Sorry you know girl's night-"

He says, "I won't keep you. Just missed you.

We need to link up boo. I was going to show up now but you busy."

"We do need to talk. Thanks for understanding, this night means a lot to Kayla and me. I really need to talk to you too. If Kayla goes home, I'll give you a call. If not, then we meet up tomorrow, okay?"

Kayla whacks my leg. She pours more wine in her cup.

Jackson says, "Sure babe. Whatever you want. I'll be up waiting..."

My phone beeps. It says, *Tyler*. I rush Jackson off the phone. "Uh, yeah sure hun. I gotta go. Love you, bye!"

I hear a faint "I love you," as I switch lines. I mouth "It's Tyler," to Kayla. She covers her mouth with her hand.

Tyler says, "Hey gorgeous. Whatcha up to?"

"Oh just hangin' with Kayla. Drinkin',

chattin', smokin' and watchin' girly movies."

"Ick. Too romantic, use condoms after, okay?" He jokes.

I laugh. "Shut up Ty. What's going on?"

"Well. Was just checkin when I can squeeze you on my calendar again."

Shit. "Tyler. Can I get back to you on that? Kinda have a busy week ahead."

He laughs. "Right, right. Work, boyfriend, and secret rendezvous... you know what? Call me back later bug-a-boo." His sarcasm is hitting a nerve.

I laugh. "Yes Tyler, I'll call your ass later. And no, you can't come join us. Enjoy whatever it is you are doing."

He cracks up and then the call ends.

Whew!

Kayla lets out a loud breath. She says, "Girl! Back-to-back!! Can I get what you got goin' on! Damn. They on you like wildfire."

I snatch the blunt out her hand. "Tell me about it. I gotta get out of this as soon as I can."

Both our phones go off and that only means one thing: Callie and Brina are texting! We make eye contact and freeze. It's like we have been busted. The girls hate when we chill without them. I tell her, "I'm not texting until you do."

She says, "Fuck it. Let them wait." We giggle in unison and tune in to *Love and Hip-Hop Atlanta*.

Chapter Thirty-Two

TYLER

I arrive at work expecting nothing but the best. I end up on the elevator with Jackson and try my hardest not to laugh at the fact that Clare was just giving me head in a hotel. He greets me first and I nod my head, say what's up. Every time I blink, I get the images of sex with Clare. I wonder if she fucks him like that. Granted, that time I seen her ride him from outside her window showed me that she can have great sex. But, to experience it! I can't help but think if she gave me first impression sex or just how she is sex.

I hadn't run into Jackson as much today, seeing as though we both had our own projects. I focused on constructing detailed contracts for our new clients, P.S. 360. They need new computers and updated software. Also, one of us is volunteering to assist students with the ins and outs of IT. I might propose that I go and take Monica with me. What she got going on with

313

Jackson, is none of my business...yet.

Upon lunch hour, I go to speak to the higher ups and seen Jackson and Monica connecting. He gave her frosty. I have some free time, so I text Janice. Clare isn't the only one I plan on fuckin'. I write,

Hey Janice, this ya boy Tyler. The sexy guy you bumped into at Central Park. I'm down to get to know you if you are.

Then I close the messages. I decide to schedule a meeting with Jackson and his new crew instead and head to my office.

I sit in my chair and almost text Clare. I'll text her later. I close my eyes, attempting a cat nap. My phone sings, "A Millie," by Lil' Wayne. This is my default for new numbers and all unassigned calls. I frown, then answer the call.

"Yooooooo Tyler! It's Julian, I changed my number last week. I fucked some crazy bitch and now she won't leave me alone," he laughs.

Goddamn. Julian is my brother. He's 28. While he has lots of street credit, his girlfriend game been crazy. Either they call him a dawg, for cheating, or they can't shake him when he's the one ready to move on. He only had one stable girl back in college, but they broke up for differences I still don't know.

I sigh. "Julian. Really nigga? This your first greeting? I told you leave them chicks alone! And next time hit me up, you know I'm in IT."

He laughs. "My bad bruh. Anyways, I'm in DC right now but, I'll be taking a break from this Criminal Law shit to come visit you and Ma. I already called Ant, Tori, and Arielle. We all gon' be up there in two days."

"Two days?! And y'all just now telling me?! Does mom know?" I put him on speaker as I send a group text. How is it that none of my brothers and sisters think to contact me before just poppin' up! Where y'all gon stay at?

My other line goes off, it's Tori. I set up a conference call just as Julian says Ant is calling him and I tell Tori to call Arielle. Now we can settle this like one big ol' family.

Tori apologizes right away. She's the baby out of all of us and gets away with everything. She says, "I knew you were busy with Jackson and trying to come up at your job. I didn't want to burden you, but the rest of 'em insisted we come. I tried telling them you got Ma, but noooooo--"

She's interrupted. Arielle says, "Ok suck up. Tori stop." She pauses, laughs. "Tyler it ain't that deep. Don't you think we should all be together anyway? Plus, we have some huge news for you!"

Tori is 30, she is a radio host in San Francisco, for Power 103.5. She and I always been close since little kids. Arielle convinced her to move to the West Coast with her so they can live the sisterly dream of jobs, boys, gossip, and relationship advice. They used to be neighbors until Tori got a job offer, she couldn't refuse. Arielle is 34, works as a celebrity journalist, living in LA.

Anthony, aka Ant, the oldest, is 36 and lives in GA, working as a chef in his own restaurant. He's been working hard at it since he was 25. I'm proud of him.

I'm 32 years old...fitting right in between all my foolish siblings. Who knew we all had successful potential in us? I was for sure Ant and Julius would be out selling and dealing the way they misbehaved in high school. My mother told me Ant used to get suspended quite often.

Their visit is a surprise for mom. They want her to feel loved and knew if I spoil it or they just call her, she will reject everyone taking time out of their lives to come check on her. I told them I will keep quiet and make arrangements for them to stay at the *Hyatt*. Everyone is belting out positives and too hype, as I tell them I have to go. We say, "I love you." The call ends and I stare into the atmosphere, wondering what's going on. Surprise can only mean a few things, marriage, baby, or new house. Shit probably all three. Well, I'll just have to wait and see.

I drink some water then get back to work. The work phone goes off and I answer it. It's Jackson telling me that I can come meet them in the conference room in 30 minutes. I say, "Ok cool," then hang up. I start playing around with this video game app I created that I plan on building to also donate to charities to fund children that cannot afford college. This will buy time until the meeting.

****

During the meeting it was hard not to think about my family coming to town. The board members approved of my proposal for the public school system updates and said I can take Monica with me. On my way out the door, I text Calli. I tell her to meet me tonight at the *Holiday Inn*. I'm not sure if she will be down for this so blunt, so fast, but it's worth a shot.

Janice message came in as well.

Hey Tyler! About time you got back to me. Let's meet up this weekend. Drinks and food then I'll see if you deserve the rest of me.

I chuckle. She's cute. I write back,

Oh, trust me baby. I know how to work my way into anythang!

There's a knock at my door and I lift my index finger to wait, as I'm wrapping up my sexual innuendos through text. I look up and it's Jackson.

"Good job on the meeting today. You're really growing here Tyler. I don't know how you do this and rideshare but you doin' it. Let me know if they need any other supplies and I'll get it sent over and approved."

I nod my head. "Thanks, my guy. I'm on it. We will head there tomorrow morning. So, when is the next party with the boys?"

He laughs. "I'm thinking this weekend. I'll hit

them up and send you a personal invite."

I say, "Sounds good to me." I stand up to leave while reading a text that says,

Whatchu' doin'? Nuttin chillin at the Holiday Inn...who you wit? Me and my people, you bring four of your friends.... LOL! Hell, yeah, I'm down to fuck and dash. Meet me right now with your fine ass.

Calli's humor is just as cheesy as Clare's, yet slightly worst. I can see why they are friends. I double check my pockets making sure I have my wallet and my keys. I turn the light off as Jackson is following behind me.

"Have a hot date, do we? I can see you're in a hurry after that booty call text," he jokes.

"Actually I do. I'm meeting with..." I pause, unsure if I can trust him with this information. Then again, Clare gave me the okie doke to meet up with her.

He says, "Aw shit. It's someone I know. Isn't

it?"

I lock my office door once we clear it and I say, "Yeah. I'm meeting up with Calli."

He is shocked. He raises his hand for a high five. "Okay now Tyler. I don't know how you did that and yet, I don't think I wanna know. Go 'head and do what you gotta do. I'll holla at you."

I smirk. "Aight playa." I tap his hand to complete the high five and then we give dap. I walk out waving bye to everyone.

Once I'm in my car, I spray some cologne and turn on music. I get to the hotel in 10 minutes. Calli is waiting in the lobby. She's wearing a little black dress, black kitten heels and a small black purse. I greet her with a hug, and she waves the room key in my face. A smile curls at my lips and before I can get a word out her tongue has met mine and my dick starts to rise. She pulls on my hand and says, "let's go." I know these women don't think they gonna keep taking control of me. I'm going to be the boss in this bedroom.

Inside the room, she locks the door. She undresses. She has on a purple bra and panties set. I chew on my bottom lip. I grab the condom out my wallet, strip my clothes off in a matter of seconds and pounce on her. We fall not so gracefully on the bed and make out. I work my way to her clit and eat like I didn't have a meal yet. She's moaning and it's fueling my excitement. A big gush of wetness exerts from her pussy, and I lick her clean. Then I lift my head up, wipe my face, and put my dick in. She shouts, "Ugh. Yes Tyler! Damn you're fuckin' big!!" I smirk and bite my lip.

Our bodies rocking in unison, the bed shaking, and it feels so damn good. Her titties are beautiful, areola's a soft, caramel complexion as I put my mouth on both of them. She curls her back. Then I lick her neck and whisper, "turnaround girl." I slide out and watch her flip over. I insert my shit back in and put that work in. Now she's yelling my name. "Tyler! Tyler! Oh Tyler!" I up my tempo, her ass clappin against my dick. Then she says, "I'm cumin'." We nut together. She collapses and I hop off her, removing the condom.

"Whew. That was goooood. I hope you gonna be ready for round two." Calli says.

I laugh. "Girl, I don't know. I'm always ready, but I have to get some work done. I left early so I can fuck you then work from home. The grind doesn't end baby."

She chuckles. "You're cute. It's a shame Clare can't have you. But maybe that's good for me."

Clare. The hairs on my back raise. I'm suddenly itchy. I must be quiet too long because Calli asks, "Are you okay? Did I say something wrong oorrr—-"

I cut her off, "Oh nah. Nothin' like that. Just got a lot on my mind. Gotta handle some business. My bad."

She is putting her bra and panties back on as she heads to the bathroom. "Okay great. Just had to be sure."

I can hear her peeing as I'm getting dressed. I shout, "You need a ride home?"

The water is running so I wait until she finishes. She walks out. "If you could? I took a cab here."

I say, "No problem boo." I finish getting dressed, dispose of the condom and notion for us to leave.

I hand the front desk the key. He smirks, staring too long as if he knows what we just did. I give a head nod and we exit the building.

As we get in my car I say, "Don't fret your little precious heart. This isn't the last time we meet. Round two will be coming up soon. Leave your schedule open."

She smiles. "Okay! So here is my address. 321 New Lots Ave." New Lots. Great.

I put on *Spotify* and take off. My phone is connected to Bluetooth to the car, and it reads, Incoming Call: *Clare*.

Calli asks if I'm going to get that. I say, nah I'll call her later. She makes a questionable face, as if she wants to pry but she doesn't. I just hope she don't go ask her why she is calling me.

Goddamn it!

I drop Calli off and tell her I'll see her later. I speed off, hitting the call button to call Clare. She answers, sounding preppy. Maybe she is drinking too much wine. Of course, I gotta toss in a casual joke when she says, "Oh just hangin with Kayla. Drinkin, chattin, smokin and watchin girly movies."

Which then I say, "Ick. Too romantic, use condoms, call if y'all need some dick after, okay?"

Kayla is her ride or die. I'm sure if we met, I'd have to pass tests to survive. I can tell my joke annoyed Clare in a good way. I want her to think about me after the call so that's all I leave it as. Busy weekend? Okay Clare boo. I know that's a goddamn lie. I'm sure she has to work but make no fool out of me. Ugh. I need a shower. I'll schedule time for a pop-up visit on babe later.

Chapter Thirty-Three

CLARE

Watchin tv and spending time with my girl is what I needed. The shame and embarrassment after cheating with Tyler has been eating me alive. Of course, work and friends help me bottle it all up. Eventually I have to face my truth.

Kayla stopping by to hear me out, has been so relieving. I will eventually tell Sabrina and Calli, but I was just not in the mood for Calli's banter. I wonder if she called him yet. I'll have to ask when we all hang out again. Brina and Calli interrupted our girl chat after we haven't responded to their texts. Calli calls me with Sabrina yellin' in the back, "Put it on speaker!"

Kayla and I shout, "Hey girls!"

Calli says, "You whores! This how it is now? Let me guess, you were lickin' clits as to why you bitches ignored our texts?" She laughs.

Kayla starts to speak but I hold a finger up. I say, "Yes Calli, sometimes we get down like that. Want to join?"

Kayla spits out her wine. Sabrina is crackin' up in the back of Calli's line. Calli laughs.

Calli says, "Ha. Very cute. Anyways. We're due for a rectangle unison. Stop this twosome shit asap. What were y'all doing anyways?"

Kayla snatches the phone and says, "We watched a movie, drank wine, and talked. But y'all! Clare had some weed!! We drunk and high ova here!"

"Oh. My. God. What the Fuck!" Calli yells.

I shush her. "Calm down girls dang. I lived a little...and?!" I put sass in my tone.

Sabrina says, "Okay so hands down I want to see this. She bailed on us last time."

Kayla says, "Soon bitches. Like tomorrow. Because tonight she's all mine."

We all laugh together. After a bunch of "Hell yeahs and fine," we all smooch on the phone and hang up.

Kayla guzzles up the rest of her wine. She says, "Babe, I love you but I'm leaving in an hour. I been here all day. Getting sick of lookin' at you. I need some D-"

I cut her off. "Just don't," I laugh. "You ain't gotta tell me twice. Plus, I have to shower and text Jackson. I may even invite him over. The more company the better..." My mind wanders off to having sex with him.

I'm at the scene where I rip his shirt off as we make out and I hear, "light up one more time."

"Damn it Kayla! You killed my dream." I joke.

"Well you can make that a reality once I get outta here! Now I'm puttin' on music. We gonna dance and enjoy this hour."

"As you wish, my mistress!" I smile. I need to

find her a great man.

****

Sure enough, like clockwork Kayla grabs her coat. The last hour felt like 30 minutes. Today has been a good time. I tell her to please get home safe.

She gives me a big hug and promises she will. She'll video me as long as I'm not naked. I slap her hair on her way out.

I say, "I love you girl. Hit me up."

She says, "I love you too."

Once my door closes, I run to the shower. I let it get steamy as I walk to the bedroom to lay out my blue nightgown and my work clothes for tomorrow with my blue matching bra and panties set. Night done; work clothes set. I can't wait to relax.

I scratch my head on my way to the bathroom. Of course, I'm itchy as I head to wash my ass. In the mirror I gaze into my eyes. I have got to do better. I laugh for no reason. Damn, I'm still high. I get in the shower and let the water arouse my body. It is soothing, calming, and hot. I should probably go to the spa. I'm more tense than I realized. I close my eyes and picture the life I want for myself...a 2-story house...husband, Jackson? kids...marriage...an upper-class job...

I wash up using *Sweet Pea*. A tear falls as I think about how crazy the past three months have been. I soak in the water some more, selling self-affirmations to my mind when I hear creaking. I pause, hold in a breath, and look around for a weapon. *Shit! Nothing of use in here!*

The sound of stomping gets louder. I squeeze my eyes closed and pray it's just Jackson playing games or my mind fuckin' with me. The shower curtain gets yanked, and I hear, "Hmmm Sweet Pea! You wear that thang that I like!"

How the hell did he get in here?

I swipe the curtain fast but I'm in the bathroom alone. I turn the shower off, grab my towel and wrap it around my waist. I grab the first thing I see that can knock someone out, the plumber.

Uneasy, I slowly stroll my hallway. I yell, "Show yourself!"

Silence. I keep walking, looking around, nervous. I'm shaking. I check my bedroom and there's a trail of clothes as if he was in my drawers. I rush to the door when I hear it slam. I replace the plumber with a knife. I breathe, count to five and grab the door handle. I quickly open the door and my hand is grabbed.

"What the fuck babe!?"

"Jackson! Oh My God!!!" I cry instantly, bawling...the type of ugly cry that will make a man turn away. But not this one. I kneel, feeling suddenly weak.

He bends down to help me. He asks, "Are you

okay? You're pretty shaken up. Here let's get you dressed."

I let him in as he carefully takes the knife out my hand, puts it back in the handle and locks the door behind us. With one hand on my back, he leads me to the room. I feel so confused. I have to text Kayla!

"My...my...my phone. Wh-wh-where is my ph-ph-phone? How did you-" I stammer.

He ignores the mess on the floor and reaches for my blue nightgown. I nod as he puts it over my head. I sit down.

Jackson kisses my cheek. "I'll get you some water. You get your mind right C." He walks to the kitchen.

I smack myself. Feeling tripped up, I search the room for my phone. I hear Jackson's footsteps, as I look up, he is waving my phone.

"Here. It was on the couch. Also, drink this,"

he says.

"Oh. Thanks. You're the best," I kiss him on his lips. So moist, so soft, taste like strawberries.

He asks, "Wanna tell me what that was about? You're pale ass shit right now-"

"Uh. I thought someone broke in. I was hearing shit while bathing. I got high with Kayla earlier, so I am sure it's just paranoia. Psshh." I wave my hand while guzzling the water. He knows me too well... I'm hoping he just let it go this one time.

He stares. He's silent for a minute then he says, "Well whatever Kayla got you smokin' let me get some!" He laughs.

"Actually I had some of your stash that you kept in the drawer, and she dosed us with her own, but I can ask her," I say, laughing nervously.

He looks at me. "You're sexy ass fuck in that gown. Come to ya boy. I'm bout' to put it on you..." He starts stripping. Clothes falling to the floor as I admire his fine physique.

I'm getting turned on by the second. I jump to him...lift my gown to where he can grip my ass, since I'm bare. I straddle him and make out with him. Our tongues playfully intertwine and rotate. I start dry humping him and he moans. He flips me on the bed. His fingers enter my pussy. A loud moan slips out my mouth. He kisses me, then kisses my neck, fingers still inside. He releases my gown off my shoulders, nibbles at my breasts, placing my nipples in his mouth one at a time. In an instant he is eating me out.

The double pleasure of finger fuckin' me and lickin' me is sending me. A euphoric feeling, I'm falling in love even more. I motion my hips to his rhythm. Then he gets up and puts his dick in me. He's on top, I'm letting him lead. Being made love to is what I need right now. We gaze into each other's eyes, hips in its own flow, sex having me beyond cloud 9.

Jackson feels so good. Yet, I feel a little guilty. Also, my mind tells me Tyler has been here and he left once he got what he wanted. I shake the thoughts and focus on the passionate love making.

After we cum together, Jackson falls asleep, and I text Kayla. I wait a few mins and no response. I'm worried. I don't stress it; she probably went to find someone to have sex with. I send a group text to the girls to meet up tomorrow. I put the phone down, snack on cheese doodles, drink some juice and get in bed next to Jackson.

****

Waking up next to Jackson feels like the good old days. I have to get ready for work. It's 7:15AM. I put on the clothes I had laid out last night. I wake Jackson with a kiss and place the spare key in his hand.

"Shit. Is it time for work already?"

"Uh yeah hun. The grind doesn't stop." I grab all my belongings.

"Hey C, let me wash my face and shit. Then I'll drive you."

"Fine! Hurry Jackson. I want to stop at Nick's before going in."

He flings the sheets off his body. Rising off the bed, he smiles. I assume that's in relation to the key and our wonderful night. He heads to the bathroom to wash up and brush his teeth.

I check my phone. No response from Kayla. Not even in the group text. If she doesn't get back to me or us by lunch, I'm stopping by. I open up IG and see Tyler's page. Soon as I plan on digging, Jackson comes out the bathroom, so I shut my phone down.

"Let's go," he says.

"With pleasure boo," I say. I lock up, then we get inside his car. I forget how nice his car feels.

The ride to work comes all too quickly. He parks in front of Nick's shop.

Jackson says, "I'll escort you, but I can't hang sweet thang. I have to get to work too. Maybe take a shower and put on new clothes at home first." He looks down.

I laugh. He opens the door for me, and we enter. Nick has a smile on his face.

"Well. Look what the wind blew in. Jackson! Haven't been seeing you much. Handsome. Need your usual?"

Jackson laughs. He says, "I'll just be grabbing an energy bar to go. Send my usual for lunch. Clare will cover it."

Nick says, "You know this one's always on me." He winks.

I laugh, slapping Nick on his arm, "Yo Nick! I told you he's off limits!"

"All candy is eye candy darling," Nick

rebuttals.

I kiss Jackson goodbye. We laugh in unison at Nick's silly self. I say, "Love you babe. Text me later!"

Jackson, now by the door, says "Love you more. I gotchu' ...enjoy your day at work."

Just like that he's gone. I turn my attention back to Nick. "Give me a cleanse please. I got high last night, and some trippy shit happened which I thought I saw him but when I opened the door it was Jackson instead-"

Nick touches my hand. "Whoa bitch. Breathe."

I do as I'm told. I say, "It's starting to be too much. I'm ending things with Ty today."

He says, "Yes girl. Do it before you end up dead."

Chills.

His co-worker hands me a medium green

drink. He says, "Here Clare. This is the Recovery Healer. It's got kale, vitamin c, mango, broccoli, orange juice, and my special Columbia energy elixir. You won't be needing coffee after this, but maybe the toilet," they both laugh.

I join in too, seeing as I did ask to be cleansed. "Ugh. Thank you!" I back away to the door, sipping. "Mhm! This is really good. You should add this to the menu. I gotta go before I'm late and they kinda know this is my first stop every time. Bye boo."

He waves.

The drink didn't even make it to B&N door because I was so thirsty. I inhaled it in seconds. I toss the empty cup in the trash and walk toward work.

Breathe. Clare, just breathe. I close my eyes.

When I open them, I'm faced by Tyler. Oh, hell no! Not this morning! I walk around him. "Excuse me Tyler! I'm late. Talk to you when I'm off...Maybe." I push past him, running to safety.

I hear a faint "No she didn't. Curb me? Blue nightgown--" he says, confidently.

I stop in my tracks. I shake my head. Can't deal with this now. I have to clock in.

Chapter Thirty-Four

JACKSON

Work has been going really well for me. After lunch, I gave Monica her frosty and that was it, just so no one talks. I'd be a fool if word gets back to Clare. I wrapped up some more coding on the website before heading home.

Once I get home I head straight for the whiskey. With a heavy mind, I sip and think about all that Clare, and I been through. That time she surprised me at work, then was all antsy then, still has me questioning what has really been going on with her. If it's any of them haunting, ghost books trippin' her up then she need to take a break from them. She almost looked like she was avoiding someone, but she only knew me there...I think? I need a refill. As I pour more whiskey into my glass, I unbutton my shirt and take off my pants. By the time I'm back on the couch, I'm in my undershirt and boxers.

I've never felt so bossed up, being one of the chairmen. Apparently, the ladies see it too. I'm not about to be that office type, the one that fucks the women for their hype. Monica is a bad bish. As the gentleman that I am, I offer to bring her a frosty because of my manners. It's a good thing we keep work at work.

I hadn't expected Clare to be so kind and loving with her texts lately, like she used to be when we met up. Of course, her suspicious actions the night before had me on edge, but she told me it was an *Uber* cab, so I have no choice but to trust her.

Even though, the driver was speeding, I prayed for her safety. That night I went home to rest my head. Over time with work, I realized if I aim to put as much effort into Clare as I did with my promotion, we would be back to our old ways.

Now when I pulled up on her, I hadn't expected her to look like she been haunted. I don't like this jumpy behavior; we need to discuss it soon. But I missed my baby, I went there to put it on her and that I did. After sex I fell asleep, everything felt like we were becoming "in love" all over again. When she kissed me, I wanted round two, but I knew we had to go.

I stopped by Nick's store for fun. His humor sets anyone up for a good day. Plus, I like free shit. I hate leaving Clare in a hurry, but I have to get to work, look over my schedule and hold meetings. A few with Monica at the table. I have to mentally prepare myself.

****

As usual work is busy. I discuss the school information with Tyler as him and Monica are going to do that in the afternoon. I also complete all my website coding and designing. But I do not want to advertise it just yet. I need to sleep on it.

Monica was sending flirty eyes during the meetings, but I kept it professional. She was going to follow me, but hesitated when my co-

344

chairman, Rolland taps my arm to speak. She walked away quietly, and I silently cheered. Plus, she need to get ready for the software and computers sent over to the public school with Tyler.

It seems as if time is flying. Everything is running smoothly. It's 4PM and I am leaving for the day. I'm checking my phone messages as Tyler approaches me.

He says, "Jackson, are we chillin' or what?"

Without looking up, I say, "I'll hit my guys up and shoot you the info. Right now, imma head out." I look up to give him a pound and exit.

In the car, I text the group chat. I ask

What's the word? I'm a free man tonight!

Then I start the car to head home. I bump some music and get interrupted by the Bluetooth stating Clare is texting. I have the read aloud on, so the message says,

Hey baby, I was wondering if we can all get together... you know my girls and your boys. Let me know! I'm tryna get in touch with Kayla...it was her idea anyway. Ok, Love you.

I smile. At the red light I reply using voice to text.

Hey babe, sure! I'll text them and let you know exactly when. Love you more.

I have an incoming call: *Mommy*. I answer it, she sounds so happy.

"Hey love. I heard from your sisters. I'm glad you all woke up out your busy lives to call one another," she says.

"Hey Ma," I reply, excitedly. I love my mama. "Yes, I finally had time after getting promoted to have life beyond work. I missed them. How are you?"

"I'm good, you know working out, loving your father, watching my shows. What's up with you?"

I laugh. "TMI about dad. I'm good. You'd be happy to know Clare and I are working through our issues."

"Oh Good! I'm glad. I love Clare. Bring her sometime," she says.

"I will Ma. Matter of fact, I'm coming over. Put some clothes on," I joke.

She cracks up. "Boy please! Stop that nonsense and come on over! See you soon, love you."

"I love you too mom. On my way."

I set the destination, roll my windows down and I'm out.

Chapter Thirty-Five

TYLER

I feel like the world's eligible bachelor. Quick, someone put me on ABC. I joke to myself. After dropping off Calli, I continue riding around. I speak to Clare and tease her on purpose. By all means, I'm not stopping sex with Calli. She's single and the sex was damn good. It was a quick fraudulent slip for Clare to call as she exited my car. She probably thinks I had that planned.

I am going work, nap, and shower so I can meet Janice. I get home in no time and walk to the bathroom to shower. I let it steam as I text Janice my address. Before I put the phone down, it vibrates. I read the message:

I was waiting for you. On my way. What should I bring? I think for a sec.

I got it! I write,

I have all you need here. Just bring that fine ass

of yours.

Then I hop in the shower. I have to wash Calli off me. I steam and wash up, remembering that I have to submit a work memo asap. I air dry, walking toward my computer.

25 minutes later, Janice rings the doorbell. I let her in. She sees that I'm naked and says, "Mhmmm! Ready and willing." Then she kisses me. Aggressive and taking change, Janice strips my towel off. She pushes me toward the couch to give me head.

I rest my hands behind my head. She's deep throating me which makes me groan. I palm her face with two hands, directing her to go moderately faster. Before I reach my edge, I release her, gently lift her off me and say, "my turn then I'm gonna bend you up."

She smiles. I lick her kitty kat for 20 minutes then I fuck her silly. We switch positions three times, ending up in the frog position. We're two yelling freaks when my bell rings and I hear a knock. I tell Janice, "Don't stop. I'm almost there. Let's go." I pound her faster.

As we are cumin' I hear, "Damn playa! Open up!" That's Ant. Then he is followed by "I know he hear us knocking," Tori says.

I say, "Shit! Janice gets dressed, NOW!"

She laughs as she puts her clothes on. I toss on my boxers, Nike shorts and a black T-shirt. I yell, "One minute you creeps!" I go in the bathroom and wash my dick off and my hands. When I come out, I kiss Janice and tell her, "That was great. We will do this again my dear. And no, you will not meet my siblings."

She says, "We sure will. I had a great time Mr. Sling-a-ling! Call me. I also, hadn't planned on it." She walks toward the door, open it and says, "Hello everyone. Sorry, excuse me."

Ant, Julian, Arielle, and Tori watch her leave as they enter my house. Ant has his hand raised for a high five. I laugh and give him a five. Julian says, "You got one for me?"

I tell him, "Nah, go find your own. NYC has plenty ladies for you." I go in the kitchen and pull out five cups, about to bartend.

Once all the whiskey sours are made, one is left sitting. Arielle says, "Bro... so here's the news... I'M PREGNANT!"

I pause in the middle of drinking. I put the cup down and say, "Whoa. Congrats sis." I give her a hug.

Tori says, "That's not all we came to tell you..."

I sit with one leg crossed over the other, waiting.

"I'm engaged! Javier comes down tomorrow. I can't wait for you to meet him!"

I blink. The ride isn't over yet as Arielle says, "Prepare for a double wedding because so am I!"

She pulls the ring out of her pocket. "We didn't want to slap you in the face with everything at once."

Ha. A pun. Little does she know we have a secret sibling...unless mom told them already..."Well then. No one likes to make calls these days. All these surprises. Interesting...does mom know any of this?"

Julian says, "Yeah bro. We just seen her before stopping by."

"Did she mention anything to you guys?" I ask, emptying my glass.

Everyone shakes their head. Only Tori says, "Nope. Why?"

I say, "Oh no worries. We'll sit with mother so she can tell you guys herself."

Worry fills everyone's faces and I say, "Round two everyone? Arielle, a mocktail?"

Everyone nods in agreement.

Ant says, "let's play Uno!!"

Tori pulls the cards out her purse and Julian sets up the table. I check my watch. I'll enjoy this family time for now. I have Clare duties in two hours.

****

Two hours later...

I send my lovely sibling on to their hotel. I tell them I have business errands to run. As we all leave my house, I lock the door and get in my car. I zoom to Clare's house. When I get there Clare is in the shower. I make noise, on purpose, to rattle her brain. I contemplate joining her. I make a mess of her home so that when she gets out, she knows it's been messed with. I inhale, *Ahhh Sweet Pea*.

I vocalize my thoughts on purpose… out loud, then I escape into the closet when I heard the front door open. I thought Jackson didn't have a key! Or did he use his IT brain and find tools to ease in. Shit. I can't remember if I closed the door all the way. That has to be it!

I see her jet out the shower in a haste, naked. The towel slips as she holds the plunger. I cover my mouth, so I don't laugh. When she sees Jackson, she's relieved, yet scared. If I know my boo as well as I been in her, I know this is a facade not to have him look at her as suspect.

Jackson's staying longer than I want him to. They make out and I roll my eyes. They shift to the bedroom. Too in tune with each other, I leave the linen closet and peek inside the bedroom. I watch them fuck for 5 minutes, just because. I don't need any tips; I just want to see how much pleasure he brings her. This is love making, make up sex.

I've seen enough. I quietly sneak out the door, leaving everything as is and collect a "hot pink bra," off the floor. When I make it to my car, I am pissed. I slam the steering wheel. My horn beeps and I curse. "Shit!" A double effect for what I just seen and the chance she knows my horn. Then a devilish grin releases as I pull away, blasting Tupac's "Changes."

The Next Day......

I tossed and turned all night, feeling betrayed. Clare IS MINE! So, what I just fucked her friend and Janice. They are side pieces. Nothing compared to her. Waking up on edge, I quickly get dressed and wash up, then I start my day with coffee. I skip breakfast to race to her job.

I had not expected Clare to blow me off. I figured she'd be happy to see me. Instead, I get "New Clare." The one who just got dicked down by her man last night. She cut me off, telling me she will talk to me later. I wanted to grab her up and stick my fingers in her coochie like last time, but after what I saw last night, I'm good.

She storms into work, and I watch her before heading to work. Trust me, I'm very angry. I'll cool down for now....

I have to figure out this Monica shit. We are on the same schedule today as we are going to finish up at the school for the computers and softwares. Maybe I'll ask her after work.

At work, I jump right into being productive as if what I just witnessed, didn't happen. When I get what looks like the change to speak to Monica, she is heading into Jackson's office. So, I figured I'll do what I do best... I'll spy and pry to see if I can get any answers from her.

I thought she would be with Jack for a while, but it didn't last long. To see a woman actively working in this business and not as an assistant is impressive. Maybe it's my family gene, we're pretty successful. I still can't get over the news of my sisters. I must have been daydreaming too long because Monica knocks asking if I'm ready to go.

I snap out of my reverie, "Let's go girl! By the way, I'm about to get to know you by asking some heavy questions so get ready while we spend all day together." I cut my office light off and lock up.

She throws an arm around me; it feels sibling like. "Ugh fine. Interrogation day it is. But you are buying coffee first!"

After Work...

The day enduring teachers and students was cool. Some little boys and girls approached Monica and I saying they can't wait to work for IT. I just laughed because it's not as easy as it seems. When Monica and I had time in between, I was asking Qs like where she is from and what's her family like. She's a city girl for sure. Based on her description of her upbringing, I can tell she has no idea what's going on. Right after we concluded our work duties, I blurted it out. "Monica, I'm not sure if you know this, but we are related."

She laughed. "Shut up. You're kidding right?"

I looked her in the eyes. I put my bag on my shoulder as I said, "Real shit. Your mother is my mother...you also have 4 other siblings."

Monica's jaw dropped. She sinks to the floor. "Please...please tell me Anthony, Tori, Arielle and Julian are.... them? My father told me they were my cousins.

"Yep....and me, of course...welcome to the family, I guess." I put my hand out to help her up. We were outside the school doors. She hesitates before grabbing my hand.

"Thanks..." she got up, dusted her clothes, and walked to the car.

I tightened my lips and silently said, "well, this is going to be awkward."

In the car her mood changed. She said, "Noooo wonder why we are big flirts!"

I turned away from her, distracting myself from being seen. She never seen me interact with

Clare, so I don't know why I'm trippin'.

She said, "Our boss. Jackson is soooo cute. I just wanna lick him up...and I see how you look at Carrie."

I laughed. The incoming call goes off in the car just as I was about to play music: *Clare*.

Monica laughs. I shush her and answer. Clare yells, "Meet me at Olive Garden, I'm at the bar!" Then she hangs up.

Monica says, "Oh you have got to fill me in now! Big brother!"

Sigh.

**** THE TALK***

I drop Monica home. Before she gets out, we exchange numbers. Technically, I already have it because I looked through the work employee contact sheet. But I play along. I have to sit on all this new information.

After the call, I filled Monica in on my intentions. She said I'm creepy, yet cute and I haven't harmed anyone yet. When she realized Clare is Jackson's girlfriend, she choked up. Not in a bad way, but her mind reeled. She then had a devious plan to play a game of operation, separation.

Monica wants in. I tell her I can't dwell on the details any further as I have to meet Clare. I take off without a formal goodbye. I meet Clare at 42nd street's Olive Garden.

She's at the bar like she said. She's singing along to the music and drinking an oversized margarita. "Call Me Maybe" by Carly Rae Jepsen is on. In her own world, I sneak up to her and whisper in her ear, "Hello beautiful." I lick it after.

She jerks, and a soft moan escapes her lips.

She swivels in the chair and pats the one next to her for me to sit. She reaches for the bartender.

I retrieve her hand and tell her to relax. The man comes over, his tag says "Jared."

She says, "He will have a whiskey shot. Top shelf."

I laugh. I plummet a kiss on her cheek. "Thank you lovely."

When the shot comes, she tells me to drink. I do as requested and also ask for another. Clare laughs. She sits up straight. Clears her throat as I watch the vein in her neck.

We spiel out how are you's and our usual banter. I can tell, this time she is stressed. I say, "Based on how you been acting boo, I will say just get it out."

She hit my arm, jokingly. Then says, "You're right. Here it goes..." she takes a huge sip of her drink. "Tyler, what we had was amazing. The sex was great, our chemistry is almost unusual. However, I love Jackson and we are working things out-"

"So you brought me here to dump me?! Great! No need to say anymore. But Clare, I do love you. You're everything I ever wanted..." I lift her chin. I draw her lips closer to mine..."You're meant to be mine. You. Me. We happened for a reason. I'm not letting up so easily." I bite my bottom lip. "Your sweet, peachy scent when you are ready to have sex is my favorite..." I'm starting to feel the whiskey.

She turns her head. "I'm sor-sorry Tyler. I really am. My heart is with Jackson. What we had was just a fling. Please don't make this harder than it already is."

I slam my hand on the table. I look around to make sure I'm not causing a big scene. A few onlookers pay me attention, but I mouth, "Sorry." The bartender, Jared hands me another drink. He mouths, "You need this." And I do. I chug it in seconds. Clare is crying.

I found the words to say, "Clare. I can't lose you. I want to be with you. I want to inhale Sweet

Pea every day and see you where red lingerie and blue bra panties set often. I know you hate waking up for work at 7am, I know you were jealous when you heard about Calli and I," Clare pauses, mid drinking. I've got her full attention now. "Oh, and Kayla, she's a fighter. That day she left your house, I wanted to see you and she gave me a hassle. I had to grab her and take her to my basement for some fun..."

She slaps me. "You're the reason my best friend hasn't been responding to my calls and texts! FUCK YOU TYLER! You little idiotic freak! I don't care about you and Calli. Kayla better be okay!"

"Why don't you go see for yourself. I sent her home the same day. Goodbye love, this ain't the end of us." I throw $50 on the bar, I say, "Be tee dubs, watch your back at the office party..." then I walk away.

Chapter Thirty-Six

CLARE

I had a hard time focusing on work today. As a manager, it's not the best to show up unfocused. My mind has recollected everything from last night. Jackson and our love making, Kayla and her silence, Tyler trying to manipulate me before work. The world is closing in on my life.

When Tyler mentioned my nightgown, I became shook. It made me think about if he been watching me the whole time. Were the flashes I seen that one time with Jackson in my home actually from Tyler? Had he been trailing me every day?! How does he have time when he has his own life.

Once I get home, I almost don't want to undress. I feel like I'm being seen. Sheepishly, I remove my clothes and change into jeans, a white tee, and my black knee length boots. I put on my

North Face as it is cold out. I head back out and go to Olive Garden.

At the bar, I waste no time drinking. I call Sabrina and she said she hasn't heard from Kayla. My anxiety is getting to me, so I keep drinking. I call Tyler and yell the location, which the reason is because I'm a little tipsy and the insurance of hearing me over the music.

While I wait, I keep drinking and the music is hitting my soul. The bartender is cute. I must tip him. Time is on my side... or not. While I'm in my own business, Tyler shows up. He whispers "Hey beautiful..." I am so turned on. I mask it by playing it cool and drinking.

We cut to the chase. When I tell Tyler I can't do it anymore, he fights back. It's as if he is begging me to stay. I freeze when he says he love me. I had not expected that. We only had sex and some drinks...how can he love me? I caught chills when he said, "Kayla...she's a fighter." I truly almost punched him.

I form tears because all of this is overwhelming. Tyler continues to try to swoon me and when I don't take the bait, he leaves. I take a deep breath. I wipe my face when he leaves. Jared sent me an Amaretto Sour. He gives me a thumbs up, I'm assuming it's free. I smile and sip.

As a distraction, I check my phone. Jackson text comes in. It says,

Babe, I'm having an office party and since I'm the boss I am inviting you, your friends and mine. Spread the word! I Love You. Party is tomorrow.

I pay my tab, tip Jared, and wobble my way out the door. I sit on a bench, consuming the air. I call Calli. She answers and I say, "Bitch. We all have to talk. Have you spoke to Kayla?"

Calli: "Uh, yeah. She sounded unlike herself. She's home resting."

"Tag Sabrina. I have an announcement. I'll call Kayla."

Calli: "Okay..." she puts me on hold.

I do the same, praying Kayla answers.

A sleepy Kayla answers. I blurt out, "Kay babe! Oh my God! I worried about you! I had nothing to do with what happened-"

She cut me off to say, "Clare. Relax. I know. Tyler been weird. I told you that. Sorry I been M.I.A. I been sleeping. I called out of work because I had a bad hangover."

"Thanks Kay. I love you! Anyways, the girls are on the other line," I say clicking to join conference.

Now that we are all together on the phone, we talk greet then I say, "Ok ok. Listen up ladies. Get your finest dresses out because my man is having an office party!! Yay!"

Kayla: "I'm down. Are his friends gonna be there?"

Sabrina: Laughs. "Kayla u horn dog. Whose

closet are we stealing from?"

Calli: "Obviously Kayla's!"

Me: Laughing. "Whew chile. Good thing y'all said her and not me! Kayla we be over there tonight."

Kayla says, "Sleepover?"

"Sure!" And "You bet," all fly from our mouths.

Chapter Thirty-Seven

TYLER

After the bar, I head home. I speed through the lights, not caring if I get a ticket. I make it home safely. During Clare's fiasco, my siblings blew me up in a group chat for a movie night. I send a quick "Sure send the details after tomorrow, have an office thing."

Ant and Julian ask to come, and I say sure. I lay down. I put the phone down, then get this urge to text Clare. I lift my body up and text,

Let me guess, you're finally home. In bed, wearing some red nightgown as you rotate from the blue one. See you soon boo.

I take my pants off and put my phone on the nightstand, ready for sleep.

*****

I wake up, ready for one last try. I quickly get dressed. I hop in my car, zooming to Nick's shop.

I sit and wait for Clare to show up. I almost go inside, but I know he's her buddy. Impatient, I keep looking from my watch to the door. She doesn't show up. I walk straight into the bookstore. I see Clare putting children's books away. I spiel, "you cannot do this! I won't let you! Give us a try..."

She yells, "SECURITY!!"

In an instant they come, grab both my arms and escort me out. My legs putting up the fight, I scuffle and drag my feet. They toggle back and forth with me, before grabbing my legs too. I yell, "Clare! This is what it is now?! Ok, watch next time I see ya!"

My phone is going off once security drops me outside. I answer without looking. It's Mom. She is yelling at me asking if I spoke to Monica because she got a call from her sister, my aunt. News travels fast!

I tell mother, "I don't have time to talk right

now. See you and the siblings at movie night. Love you!"

I end the call and go to work. I'm ready to have some drinks, good food and get to know the other employees while I pretend, I don't have ill intentions when my guest of honor arrives.

Chapter Thirty-Eight

JACKSON

In life they tell you when things are looking too good, something bad is about to happen. It felt good seeing mom. She always gives me some wisdom. She told me my sisters will be in town soon and she cannot wait. They went on a vacation the Bahamas and Florida and return in three days. I got a haircut from Sal before heading home.

I'm also thrilled Clare wants her girls to meet my boys. I'm hoping a love connection goes down. I purchased a Gucci suit on my way back from my mom's house just for the office party. Which I text Clare about, so it knocks two or three birds with one stone.

Sleep has been few and far between for me lately. So many occurrences for me. Tyler and Monica had a great day at the school, my coding for the company website and my own is succeeding and I hope to launch my company tonight. The main goal of this office getup is a celebration. I am leaving to start my own shit.

*****

It's party time! I wake up feeling like Usher, "U Don't Have to Call." After my shower, I did the same exact slide to my clothes. The suit is gold and black, I'm wearing a white button up and a gold tie with a shiny black handkerchief and gold shoes. I am wearing Usher's V.I.P. as well. I look at myself in the mirror. I look good and feel good. I text Clare.

Can't wait to see you.

I drive to work. I park in my now, "boss spot." I greet the employees on my way in. Before handling some quick work, I deal with the first one, Monica. In my office, I call for her to come see me.

Instantly she arrives. Not allowing any physical touching, I tell her I have to end things.

Monica makes a face. "This is a waste of time." She folds her arms.

"I'm sorry dear. I was at my lowest. My girlfriend has been acting weird, we were fighting all the time. It shouldn't have happened. However, I do like working with you."

She rolls her eyes. Her attitude is like.... Tyler's. I scratch my chin. My thoughts are interrupted by the sound of crashing. This bitch just knocked my desktop off the desk! She winks on her way out.

My assistant Carrie runs in after her asking if she can help me. I say, "Please have maintenance come pick this up. Also schedule me to order a new one. I'm heading to the party spot for a whiskey sour." I push away from the desk, standing up.

She says, "Of course, I'm on it."

I look back and say, "Oh and Thank you."

On my way downstairs to the lounge, I call Q. I fill him in on what just happened. He is laughing.

Q says, "Bro. I told you chicks are crazy! You did the right thing. Go back to slangin' Clare. She fine as hell anyways. Let me get dressed so I can link up wit'chu early."

"Aight bet." I laugh and hang up. I walk in and it's me and another worker there. I take some pics and send them to Clare. I write,

Waiting on the love of my life to enter the building. Don't I look dashing? Or how they say it in them sex books you read? I look the fuck good girl!

I chuckle. I scroll *Facebook* as the room fills. Tyler approaches me, "Lookin good playa'. Is it your birthday or sumthin'?" He teases.

"Nah. But tonight, is a big deal for me. You'll see."

He says, "Word. And I'm lookin forward to

seeing my new friends..."

I shake my head. He walks away to mingle.

The DJ puts on Jay-Z "Big Pimpin'." Now everyone I work with has entered the room.

Chapter Thirty-Nine

CLARE

It's still tough thinking about what Tyler did to Kayla to get under my skin. I'm so glad she didn't take it out on me. I need to call my mom before feeling up for this party.

I search my closet, in hopes to find something useful to wear. I come across a red mini skirt. I put it on and throw on a white blouse. It matches my white lingerie set underneath. I find some panty hose in my drawer and put them on. I'm going to wear slippers to Kayla's house because she has better heels.

While looking under my bed for my slides, I hear a clanking noise that sounds like it's in the kitchen! I pop up quickly, tiptoe to the area. It's empty. I sigh, in relief. Then something falls out of my medicine cabinet in the bathroom, causing me to scream. I go pick it up, it's Advil.

Nice try Universe! I don't need this...yet. I put

my ID, keys, pepper spray, nail filer and lipstick in my red clutch. I call my mom. I brief her on what's been going on and she yells at me for betraying Jackson.

She says, "I'm disappointed in you babe. I thought you knew better! Don't make the wrong choices with men. I have been there before dealing with your father. Don't let sex cloud your judgment! Jackson is a wonderful man with a great job and from the looks of you... amazing sex!"

I whine, "You're right mom. I apologize." I try not to choke up. I refuse to cry! I explain, "Mom I know. He forgave me! I'm working on it."

She says, "Yeah girl, don't lose out on that good man. He was going to marry you! Sit on that. Apologize to him, not to me baby."

I say, "Yes mom, I'm on my way to his office party now.

She gets excited, giddy. "Well go on then baby! Call me later. I love you."

I laugh. "I love you too mom."

I feel nauseous. I rush to the bathroom. I think I need to eat, could be stress. I dry heave over the toilet just as I hear Kayla yelling at my door. Nothing comes out so I throw water on my face.

I grab my clutch, and phone, then I open the door. She grabs my keys, locks the door, and pulls me away. She says, "You ok girl? I heard screams and it almost sounded like you were about to vomit...need a Gatorade?"

"Anxious much Kayla? Damn! I'm okay. I am probably just thirsty and starving!"

She laughs, still pulling me, she says, "I'm ready to partay!" She tells me the girls are at her house already picking outfits, except for Abby. She had to leave town for a family emergency. Kayla looks at what I'm wearing while we are in the car. "Cute skirt, but I'm changing your top."

"Heeyyy what's wrong with what I have on?" I whine.

She giggles. "It's cute... for a parent teacher conference, not for the CEO's woman!"

I pout. "Fine."

"And I assume you wore slippers so you can wear one of my pumps?" She says.

"Yes, my love. To look my best is to explore the best closet in town," I taunt.

She pinches my cheeks. Then she puts music on a we head to her house. The song, "Not Tonight (Ladies Night)" by Lil' Kim Feat. Da Brat, Left Eye, Missy Elliott & Angie Martinez comes on and we sing along.

At Kayla's house and the girls are dressed. Sabrina settled for a little black dress with yellow stilettos and Calli has on a navy-blue top with a black skirt and blue Manolo's. Kayla looks at them, snapping her fingers. "Yeessss bitches!!"

She leaves the room and I say, "We are going in there strong girls! Hot tamales!" We all laugh.

Calli says, "Clare, there's something I have to tell you..."

Kayla is back just in time with a tray, and she yells, "SHOTS!" We each grab one. It's clear, so I'm sure it's vodka. Kayla says, "I opened the Belvedere! Cheers!"

We clank cups and then Calli presses on. "I slept with Tyler!"

I almost choke on the vodka as it is going down my throat. "Psshhh C. I knew that already! Ty loves to brag about his lady lineup." Sabrina and Kayla are speechless.

Calli asks, "Sooo you're not mad? Or...or jealous?"

I wave my hand dismissively. "No girl. We

had a fling or two. I ended that already. He's yours if you want him, I'm staying with Jackson." I look at Kayla for the shirt I'm supposed to change into, and she nods.

Calli jumps up to give me a hug. Kayla and Sabrina joins in. Calli says, "Ugh. I love you, Clare! I was so worried it will ruin our friendship! I saw your face the day I took his card."

Kayla laughs. "You know Clare don't like to share. But I'm not letting her let that fine ass man Jack, go off in them streets. I gave her a wake up call...now let's smoke real quick." She waves four blunts in the air, which I just noticed was also on the tray.

"Shit, ain't gotta tell me twice!" Sabrina says.

Then Kayla leaves the tray on the bed and goes in her closet for the shirt. She comes out with a white blouse with black polka dots. It looks like a belly top. I take the shirt from Kayla and remove mine, putting it on. As I said, it comes down to midriff. But it looks cute with the skirt. I give her a thumbs up.

Calli and I reach for a blunt at the same time. She laughs and hands me one. "My pleasure," she says before I can speak.

I smile. We all inhale and crack up. After a couple minutes of smoking and tossing ideas about how we want the night to go, I say, " I look at them and say, "Can we go now gals!? I think Jackson has a speech and I want to be early."

We gather our things and head out the door. Sabrina still has her blunt in her hand. She says, "Oh I'm going to finish this."

We pile up in Kayla's car. I'm in the passenger seat. After applying more lipstick, I text Jackson,

Hey babe. We are on our way!

The guilt is still burning me up inside, so I text Tyler,

I'm hoping we can be friends.

Kayla says, "Stop texting your hoes and put the phone down. We will be there soon."

We start jammin' and I pry into Sabrina business. Girl chat is exactly what we need. Sabrina says, "Dang y'all nosy! FYI, I am dating a doctor from Stony Brook and the sex is AMAZING!" She dances.

I hug her. "I am so happy and hype for you girl!"

Calli: Okay now! She is getting that medical dick and want to show out on us! Facts girl. I see you."

Sabrina: "Yeah, I wanted it to become more official before I spoke about it. I don't like playing games anymore."

Kayla: "Word. I am with you on that. PERIOD POOH!"

****

Kayla parks in the lot as instructed. We walk

in the building and get on the elevator to go to the party. Once we reach the floor, Sabrina says, "Yeesss to this music! I'm going to find a man to dance with. I'll behave Clare." She laughs as she walks away.

Calli says, "I'm going to the bar. See ya."

I shake my head. The room is so gorgeous. I take it all in. The people, the music, and I search for Jackson.

Kayla puts her hands on my shoulders, "You alright? I'm going to mingle with Jackson's fine ass friend Q."

I say, "Yes. I think. You go ahead. I'm going to find Jackson." My nerves are shaking. She leaves me. Now I'm alone. I don't see Tyler, so I guess that's a good thing. I close my eyes and breathe...hands wrap around eyes. I panic.

"Yoooo what's good lil' sis!" Fuckin' Mark!

I sigh, part relief, part annoyed. "Hey Mark!

What's up?"

He says, "Ain't shit. Chillin' watching how my boy Jackson has come up. I'm proud of him ...and you." He says, embracing me in a hug.

Feeling awkward, I hug him back. "Thanks, me too. Where is he by the way?"

He says, "I'm not sure. I think he went to his office."

"Okay I'll go find him."

"Want me to come with you?" He asks.

"No I got it. Enjoy the party," I say looking around. I walk around the office area. I see some woman straightening herself up. She's looking in the reflection of an office window adjusting her dress, showing more boobs and ass. I start to feel sick again. I slide down to the floor, take breaths. I need a croissant or something.

"Need a hand?" It's the voice of a woman.

I stall before grabbing hers. "Thanks. I should go get something to eat."

She says, "Drinking and smoking with no food girl? Come on let's go."

I introduce myself. "I'm Clare."

She says, "I know who you are. I'm an employee here. My name is Monica."

"Ah. I see." We head in the direction of the party.

Suddenly, I feel hands wrap around my waist. A mantra in my head says *please be Jackson!*

I hear, "Oouu you look wonderful tonight, baby." *Whew! Jackson!*

He sees Monica and says, "Thanks I got it from here."

She walks away, more pep in her step than needed. I raise my eyebrows, but I'm distracted by Jackson's warm lips on mine. I kiss him back so passionately.

We lock hands, and he says, "Come on I have a speech now and I need you on stage with me. I nod. Then I follow his lead.

The place really filled up. As we walk toward the stage our friends follow us to stand in front. I lowkey look around for Tyler. He is nowhere to be found. I wink at my girls as we arrive on stage. Jackson steps to the podium and he says, "Thank you everyone for showing up. We have some huge things coming for this company. I won't make this long so y'all can get back to dancing and becoming friendly.... I'm leaving next month to start my own company..."

Gunshots go off....my right arm feels warm, ears are ringing. I fall to the ground, head hitting the side of the podium-

Jack...son...I can't die. Not now!

Chapter Forty

TYLER

After speaking to Jackson, I went into hiding to prepare for my biggest night ever. Monica came to keep me company also to tell me she is falling for Jackson even though she only gave head. I told her I can tell by the way she looked at him. Then I told her don't fret because I'm in love with Clare. But she rejected me, and I hate rejection. Monica goes over to my mini bar and pours us some whiskey. We clink glasses as I tell her I'm up to a malicious plan. She's either with me or against me.

She says, "I'm with you bro."

*****

I saw Clare pass my office looking for him. I could have killed her then. Instead, I stay hidden with my lights off. Monica went out there as a friendly decoy to help her. What happened next, I didn't expect. Jackson surprised Clare on his way back to the party. Crushing my sister's heart in the meantime was not making me happy.

I toss my shot glass on the floor and open my safe, ready to make my move. I put the bullets in my Glock. I drink the bottle of whiskey, letting it burn my insides. All I feel is remorse.

If I was going to do this right, it had to be right on time. I walk into the party just as Jackson starts speaking.

"Thank you everyone for showing up. We have some huge things coming for this company. I won't make this long so y'all can get back to dancing and becoming friendly.... I'm leaving next month to start my own company...This has been a huge learning experience…"

I'm hiding on the left side, in the back. I see Monica with a butcher knife on the right side at the other end. When Jackson says he is leaving, I run to the front and aim fire. The crack of the gun is louder than the bass of the speakers.

Monica detoured and ran out the room along with everyone else scared. Only two people who didn't duck were Q and Mark. They head to the stage. Just as I quickly make my exit.

I told you Clare, you are supposed to be mine. I meant every word. You should be lucky the bullet didn't pierce Jackson right in his mouth. I aimed for you because you hurt me. Now you will feel how I feel boo...

Later Sweet Pea.

EPILOGUE

JACKSON

The speech took a turn for the worst. The party wasn't supposed to be this way. After everyone cleared out, me and the crew along with Clare's friends rushed Clare over to King's County Hospital. I went in the ambulance truck and everyone else followed in cars.

I cried the entire time, speaking to her hoping she can hear me. She wasn't breathing or moving. We all sat in the waiting room and waited. Doctor Clark came to the lobby 2 hours later and told me she's unconscious and they have to remove the bullet which will take some time including recovery. She says, "You guys are more than welcome to stay; however, I advise going home to get some rest."

"Thank you doctor, but no offense. I am not leaving my woman!"

Doctor says "Alright. Well. There's one more

thing...She's pregnant! So, congrats are in order. Now if you don't mind, I have to return."

I nearly fall to the floor.

Q and Mark ask if I'm good. Sal pats my back.

"I'm good y'all." I turn to Dr. Clark. "Wait! Can I see her?"

The doctor says, "Sure."

I walk into Room 202. She looks as if she is resting peacefully. I wonder if she is having any dreams.

"Clare..." I start before sitting down next to her. I grab her hand. "Baby we're gonna get through this. This was all just a test. I'm not innocent either. I don't want to know what you did with Tyler, and I don't care. I hope he gets some real karma... anyways..." I wipe the tears falling from my eyes.

I put my hand in my pocket, pulling out a new ring. "The speech was supposed to end grand for us. So, I'll just put this ring on your finger because I want you to be my wife. I love you, and the babies you are carrying too."

Behind me, Kayla and Q are clapping. I notice they are holding hands. They rush up to me and give me a hug.

Kayla starts crying. She says, "That was beautiful!"

I smile. I look at Q. "Yo when did this happen?"

He laughs. "At the party. We vibed right away and I told her we can kick it."

I give him a five. The doctor comes in and tells us visiting hours are over.

ONE WEEK LATER

I've been by Clare's side every day. I'm fact, I took off for a week so she's my only priority. I ordered her flowers every day, the room is filled with roses, daisies, sunflowers, and lilies. There are shades of pink, purple, yellow and orange. I sing to her daily. I also hum the melody to "Sexy Love" by Ne-Yo.

Kayla comes by after work, she brings lavenders. She happens to hear me singing every time. It almost made her cry. She updates Sabrina, Abby and Calli when they can't make it.

It's Tuesday and I'm here with all her homegirls. I was talking to Kayla about wedding plans when we all hear, "Ow. Hey... Wedding?"

I rush by her side. I kiss Clare on the cheek. "Baby you're here! We're here! Look at your finger by the way." She is blinking, trying to regain herself back to normal.

She looks at her left hand. She's cheesin' real hard. "Thank you, baby.... YES!" She tries to sit up. I tell her to relax and kiss her hand as a teardrop falls and lands on hers.

Kayla is sniffling, blowing her nose. She says,

"Sorry. Don't mind me, I am just so happy she's okay!"

The doctor comes in with the sonogram machine. She puts gel on Clare's stomach. Clare, shocked says, "Wait!"

The doctor says, "You're two months pregnant miss. With twins."

She looks at me with tears. "I-I-I..."

I say, "One step at a time baby"

TWO MONTHS LATER

CLARE

It's wedding day! Once I did physical therapy and could move just fine on my own, we set the date. It's now time!

My dress is custom made to fit over my growing belly. It's lavender and lace, belly open and it trails down to my ankles. I wanted a train but didn't feel like having the anxiety of not falling. I have on these three-inch white heels.

Kayla surprised me with a ring on her finger as well the week I got home from the hospital. She said her and Q feel like soulmates, and they don't want to wait. It's her wedding day too, it's been our dream to have a double wedding.

Kayla has on a soft pink silk dress with pink three inch heels to match. Oh, get this, she's pregnant too! Her belly is also out. Her and Q are moving fast, but she's happy. Our kiddies can grow up together!

I asked what happened to Tyler and Kayla said Calli used him sexually then tied him up until he confessed everything. He told her Monica and him are siblings. Once she heard that shit, she burned his arm with a cigarette and told him to leave. I guess him and Monica went into hiding because they don't even work at Jackson's old company anymore.

I'm flawed but I'm glad Jackson stayed by my side. I'm staring in the vanity mirror; I smile at myself. Kayla comes over and hugs me gently, since we have make up on. Our mothers walk in and ask if we are ready.

I grab Kayla's hand and say, "Ready."

Our fathers are standing at the aisle waiting to walk us. Our lovely men are at the altar, tears coming down their faces while we bee bop down the aisle to "Nothin' on You," Bruno Mars and B.O.B.

Okay! They better had been crying or else we would turn this thing around! I look in the aisle seats and do a double take. I could have sworn I just seen Tyler. I squeeze Kayla's hand, relax with this plastered smile on my face and stare into the teary eyes of my husband because I am now becoming Mrs. Clare Miller.

THE END

About the Author

Eliza Rose Eliza Rose is from Brooklyn, New York City. She is a lovely mother of two, her son & daughter. She has her Bachelor's and Master's of Arts in English, Creative Writing. She likes to read in her spare time and write on her personal blog. It has always been her dream to work in publishing and now she is living up to her goals writing romance and erotica novels. Entertaining readers, not just reading for entertainment. Stay and watch as her ideas grow into unique characters, plot twists and enjoyable love scenes.

Stay Updated for upcoming projects and socials:

https://linktr.ee/AuthorElizaRose

Made in the USA
Columbia, SC
09 November 2024

46058007R00217